Gothic High

Allan Lacoursiere

And the Pens of John Paul II

ISBN: 9798831112245
ISBN-13:

Chapter 1

Gregorian chanting rose to fill the chamber as the old grandfather clock in the corner made its presence known. Portia opened one eye and groaned. She hated to get out of bed before eighteen chimes and glared over at the clock. Not even the sun was foolish enough to get up at this hour, first day of school or not.

"Will you shut up already!" Portia snapped.

Ignoring her protests, the grandfather clock raised its voice and chanted even louder. Or so it seemed to the suffering girl. Portia blew a long black hair out of her eyes and climbed to her elbows, glaring unhappily at the grandfather clock that continued to chant. There was no avoiding getting up now, and the clothes she had selected for her first day of school lay on a nearby chair, staring at her accusingly.

"Okay, okay," she complained. "I'm up already."

She rolled out of bed with a groan and staggered towards the bathroom. Vacation was over and her first year of high school had started and already she felt as if her entire world had been turned upside down. Hot water soon steamed up the room. As Portia climbed out of the shower, a message appeared on her steamed mirror – your school bus leaves in fifteen minutes. Towelling quickly, Portia rushed into her bed chambers and quickly got dressed. Even when she got up long before the witching hour, she still managed to run late, and today of all days she could not afford to miss her bus. Not on the first day at a new school.

Her bag was waiting for her at the door like a puppy excited at the prospect of a walk. It tangled itself around her legs, nearly tripping her. "For Alphora's sake! What else can go wrong? I don't know why I bother keeping this old thing."

Still flustered, Portia snatched her bag and raced from her quarters, leaving the door ajar on her dash to the bus stop. School buses were a new experience Portia was not sure she would like. First, Portia hated getting up so early, and second, she did not know any of the others who were racing to catch this same bus. She would much rather be with the friends and colleagues she knew than have to get to know a horde of strangers. Especially on her first day in a new world. Already, she could see that two others were at the bus stop waiting, and neither one looked promising.

Pretty boy looked like a character from one of those teenage vamp novels, all chiselled features, over-developed pecs, and the arrogance of someone who knew their looks could get them anything. He flashed Portia a toothy grin that she returned with a half-smile of her own, knowing she would not be impressed with him no matter how pretty his eyes. She had found that boys like him were nothing but muscle and teeth, and when it came to assignments tended not to pull their own weight. Besides, he would flirt with anything vaguely female and hope to skate by on his charm. Altogether not her type.

The ghost was worse than a goth with its pale skin and black circles around his eye. His kind never took anything seriously. Portia wondered why anyone would allow someone like him into an important program like this. Everyone was lowering their standards these days, and when Portia saw the third member running to catch the bus with her blonde hair flailing about like a rat's nest and her bag trailing behind her, she knew nothing was truer. Lycanthrope. Back in her mother's day they never would have let one into school, and neither of these two would have been allowed to ride on the same bus as any of the others. It was a short-yellow bus or nothing.

"Oh, I made it," Lacy breathed as she caught up with the others. "I was so afraid I would miss the bus, especially when I couldn't find my brush. I must have searched everywhere for it, and wouldn't you know, I was sitting on it the whole time. How silly, don't you think?" The girl paused for a breath, and then added as an afterthought, "I'm Lacy, by the way."

"Portia," the other girl said with a polite nod.

"I'm Rhys." And the pretty boy gave them a

toothy smile.

"And I'm Ooooh-ha-ha-oooo," the second boy gave a long undulating wail, then said, "but you can call me Sayd."

Portia and Rhys gave a polite half-smile and Lacy broke out in a full-throated giggle, covering her mouth with one hand.

"You're so funny," Lacy said, pointing. "Is that our school bus?"

A yellow bus came rocketing up the street in a cloud of black smoke and dust, racing directly towards them at such speed that all four stepped back away from the curb. It squealed to a stop, burning rubber splashing off all four wheels. The bus lurched forwards and clunked backwards, rocking from side to side as the door flew open. All four crept forwards and peeked inside. The driver was an emancipated man, all skin and bones with a rictus smile and a shock of red hair that made it seem as if the top of his head had caught fire.

"All aboard," the driver cried. "Next stop John Paul Secondary School."

Reluctantly, Portia followed the others up onto the bus. Thinking, so this is a school bus, she found a seat near the back of the bus, seating herself well away from the others. Sayd and Lacy chose seats near the front of the bus, and Rhys chose to sit somewhere in the middle.

"Here we go!" The driver cackled. "Everyone buckle up and hold onto your seats."

Buckle up, Portia thought, panicked. Where is the seat belt? Suddenly the bus leapt off the ground and she was thrown back hard against her seat, the skin of her face pulled backwards by the g-forces and her teeth threatening to rattle out of her mouth. On either side long white streaks of light stretched across a purple-blue background, giving Portia the illusion she was slowly sliding back out of the bus. Her bag slid from beneath her feet, joining the other three huddled against the rear emergency door. And ahead, the other passengers seemed on the verge of following their luggage. An avalanche of flesh threatened to bury her alive and there wasn't a thing she could do about it.

"Here's your stop!" The driver called.

Suddenly the bus went into a nosedive. Portia came flying out of her seat. She landed in the heap of limbs and bodies at the front of the bus, their bags slamming into her and her fellow riders with a hard thud. The door flew open and the bus tilted to the right. Portia was in free fall, a tree rushing up to meet her. A leafy branch slapped her in the face. Somehow she managed to twist out of the way, threading the fork of two branches. And then the ground punched her breath from her.

"Is everyone all right?" Portia lifted herself face from the ground, spitting out grass and leaves as her bag thudded into her back with force.

"If this is what it's like to ride a school bus," Lacy moaned, "I don't know how the humans do this every morning."

"They did warn us that this would be a low altitude insertion," Rhys said.

Struggling to her feet, Portia said, "come on, we need to get inside before anyone sees us."

Rhys reached down and helped her up. Nodding

her thanks, Portia brushed leaves and grass from her uniform – a kilt skirt in reds and blacks, a maroon shirt with the school crest, and a pair of black leggings. Together they started across the driveway towards the front doors, when looking up, they all came to a halt in the middle of the road. The school stood staring back at them. Early morning sunlight shone off the solar panels and the upper windows. Below the glare, letters spelled out John Paul II Secondary School, and finally a row of seven doors. Everywhere was glass and brick and shiny newness.

"It's so shiny," Lacy breathed.

"What is it made of?" Sayd asked.

"Bricks. They're called bricks," Portia replied.

"If you ask me," Rhys said, "it's creepy. Give me good, honest stone and that lived-in look any day. I bet there isn't an honest cobweb within a mile of this place."

"Well," Portia gulped. "We're not getting anything done standing out here gawking. Let's get inside and out of sight."

And quickly wished she had kept her mouth shut. Reluctantly, Portia found herself leading the others towards the door. She had heard that Human buildings were haunted by the spirits of the unborn, who possessed the unwary and tormented their souls. But the sky was growing lighter by the minute, and soon the staff and students would start to arrive. She and her companions had to move into the school and get out of sight until the halls started to fill up and they could blend in with the crowds. Until then, they had to find a place to set up their lair, somewhere out of the way where they could slip in and out without being seen. They had spent hours over the past week studying blueprints, memorizing the layout of the school, but now that they had arrived everything she had learned seemed to have flown out of Portia's mind. All she could think about is one of the stairwells, or maybe the greenhouse up on the second floor, although she was not sure exactly where it was. Everything was just so different here in the Human world.

The doors were locked, as they always were before seven in the morning. Ignoring both doors and locks, Sayd stepped into the building, a whirlwind of dirt and leaves following him inside. Turning back, he opened the door for the others.

Inside, they paused to study the atrium.

"It's so clean," Lacy breathed. "There's not a cobweb or a spider anywhere."

"It gives me the HeebyJeebies," Rhys shuddered. "It's all so new. Do you think anyone has ever been inside?"

"Maybe we're the first," Portia breathed.

"I can fix it," Sayd offered, puffing himself up.

Portia curled her fingers and zapped him. "Oh, no you don't. We're supposed to blend in, so no poltergeist nonsense until we get back home."

"Spoilsport."

They were still standing inside the doors when a voice called out from somewhere in the school. "Hello, is anyone there?"

"Quick, someone's coming," Portia whispered.

"Where?"

Portia pointed straight ahead. "There."

The door straight ahead led into the library. The

four raced across the atrium, arms popping out the side of their bags to lift themselves from the ground and chase after their masters on tiny legs. Here too, the door was locked and once again Sayd stepped through it and let the others inside. The automatic lights flicked on, startling all four of them. Everywhere were windows. Behind them, they could hear footsteps approaching. In a panic, Portia led the way to the left, where a wall formed a corner as the room opened up into the main stacks. While out of sight of the doors, there was no place to hide here, and again windows looked into the room from every direction. Immediately around the corner was a mobile bulletin board with the words Pens of John Paul II splashed across its top. Portia pulled the others in behind it, where they crowded together and crouched down to hide.

"Now what?" Rhys hissed.

"Quick," Portia reached for her bag, "help me set up our lair."

Portia searched through her bag, half pulling out sweaters and books. "Give it to me, now!"

"No, mine," her bag croaked, trying to duck out of her reach.

"If you don't give it to me right this instant," Portia threatened, yanking the bag back to her side by one of its handles, "I'll turn you into a pair of shoes and give you to a leprechaun!"

The bag spat. A golden pyramid flew through the air and hit Portia in the nose. Closing the bag's mouth with a vicious pull on its drawstrings, she snatched up the object. Setting it on a shelf behind a book on the history of house paint, and a second entitled The Joys of Knitting, Portia twisted the top of the pyramid and hastily punched the symbols that made up the combination with nimble fingers. There was a brief flash, and suddenly an iron door framed by limestone blocks appeared on the door.

"Hurry," Rhys urged, pulling Portia inside.

A janitor with a fringe of grey hair stepped into the library moments after the four stepped in through the door. Scratching his bald head he called, "hello. Hello, is anyone here?"

Cleaning his glasses with a handkerchief, he shrugged. He could have sworn he had seen a group of kids come into the library.

The interior of the lair looked remarkably similar to the one Portia and her teammates used back at the Academy. Off the doorway were an open concept living room and kitchen, with two bedrooms attached to the back of the living room. Portia would be sharing a room with Lacy, while the two boys would share a second, and she suspected neither she nor Rhys would be happy with their room assignments. Already she missed her best friend, Reagan, who had not been chosen for this mission. It would be the first time the two girls were apart since their first year at the Witches Preparatory School. Sighing discontentedly, Portia made her way towards the kitchen with the other three drifting across the room in her wake.

"Hello there," an appliance at her elbow piped up. "I'm the Mixmaster 2000. Can I interest you in a beverage? I have a wide selection in my drink menu."

"No thank you."

"It's because I am only a series 2000," the little appliance pouted, "and not a series 5000."

"No," Portia protested, "I'm just not thirsty."

"We have a series 8000 at home," Lacy said. "I miss the little guy."

"There's a series 8000," the Mixmaster wailed. "Oh, I am growing more obsolete by the second. The sales fairy said they should have taken the full option package, but no! They did not even spring for the extended warranty."

"Oh, alright," Portia sighed. "I'll take a pickle juice and lemon peel cooler."

"Right away mistress!"

The Mixmanner began humming and hawing, steam rising from its corners. Peeking up at her with one eye, it said. "Uhm, could you repeat your order please."

"A pickle juice and lemon peel cooler."

"Coming right up!"

The little unit began humming and steaming at full power, adding a droning wail now and again to let Portia know how hard it was working. Soon a bell sounded, and a small door slid aside, revealing a clay mug. Portia reached out and lifted it to her lips absentmindedly.

"Ouch!" She picked a prickle out of her lip. "What is this?"

"A cactus and hot mustard smoothy," the Mixmaster piped up. "Exactly what mistress ordered."

Portia set aside the mug with a scowl. She hated cactus. She and her new team had arrived in the human world unseen and relatively unscathed.

Now all she had to do is complete her mission without getting killed or poisoned by the appliances. Portia wondered if humans still burned witches at the stake, and then decided it might be preferable to a cactus and hot mustard smoothy.

Chapter 2

"Hey, Legacy!" Rhys called. "Do you know what this Math is?"

Portia turned, angry. Her mother was the Esmeralda, the witch who had led the famous raid to recover the Eye of Destiny from the British crown jewels as they lay secure in the Tower of London. Her mother was something of a celebrity amongst the agents of the Recovery Bureau, and Portia had lived within her shadow from her earliest years. And her father had led the high council for three consecutive terms. It was hard to be the child of famous parents, and the kids often ridiculed her every success.

"Look who's talking," Portia sneered. "What are

you, the fourteenth or fifteenth Romanov to attend the academy?"

"I only have twelve older siblings," Rhys sniffed. "Besides, I only want to know what Math is?"

"I believe it's got to do with the human's alphabet," Sayd said. "You know, A B C and X. Oh yeah, and Y."

"No it's not," Lacy laughed. "It's got to do with numbers. You know, adding and subtracting."

"Adding and subtracting what?"

"Numbers, of course, silly."

"Why?"

Lacy paused, a puzzled expression on her face. "I think it's some kind of Human magic. But what it does, I can't figure out."

"Humans," Rhys shrugged. "I got Math for first period. I hope I can fake it enough to fool them."

"Just do what the others do," Lacy suggested. "That's what I always do."

"And how does that work out for you?" Sayd asked curiously.

"Very well," Lacy paused, "although sometimes I think not everyone is very nice to me. They like to point out that I am the first werewolf to attend the Academy, and I don't think they mean it as a compliment."

"At such a prestigious institution like the Academy," Sayd replied sarcastically. "I'm shocked."

Having taken the first sip of her arsenic and lemon peel tea, Portia turned to study her companions. Dressed in a tartan skirt and a white blouse, with a maroon sweater tied around her neck, she was dressed in the uniform worn by the students of this Human school. Not so her companions.

"What are you wearing?"

"A uniform, of course," Lacy laughed.

The young werewolf was dressed in a French Revolutionary uniform complete with a tri-corner hat adorned with an ostrich feather. Rhys, putting on a bearskin hat, replied. "A uniform. Don't you remember our briefing?"

Portia turned. At least the red of his British uniform was close to the colour of the school uniform. She turned a jaundiced eye on Sayd, who wore a Swiss uniform with pants that ballooned at the hip, and some kind of stripped leggings, topping the whole outfit off with what looked to her like an iron pot.

"Not a uniform, you morons," Portia sighed, throwing up her hands. "But the uniform. The ones they gave us that look something like this."

She held up the ends of her skirt before throwing up her hands in disgust.

"We don't have to wear a skirt, do we?" Rhys asked.

"Ugh!" Portio screamed. "Yours had pants, remember. I'm sure they are somewhere in your bags. Go change and quick, or we will be late."

While Portia was waiting for the others to change the Mix Master 2000 began to pester her. "Can I get you a hairball tea?"

"No thank you," Portia sighed, "I just had one."

"How about a cactus and hot mustard smoothy," the Mix Master urged. "It is important to start the day with a full stomach."

"Oh, okay," Portia conceded. "I'll have another arsenic and lemon tea."

The Mix Master hemmed and hawed, screwing up its lights to show it was working hard at the task. From time to time, steam spurted out its top in a quick hiss. When he was satisfied he had created enough noise to impress his user, he poured a steaming liquid into a mug.

"Here you are!"

Absently, Portia picked up the mug and took a large swallow. Spitting it back out and waving a hand at her burnt tongue, she cried, "Ah! Hot! Hot!"

"Is something wrong, mistress?"

"I murt my thongue," Portia cried.

"Ah," the Mix Master nodded. "You should never gulp your tea. It's hot!"

When the others came out from their rooms in their proper uniforms Portia was still dancing, trying to put the fire on her tongue out by waving her hand at her mouth.

"What's wrong?" Lacy asked.

"I murt my thongue!"

"Oh dear," the Mix Master said. "Perhaps I put a little too much battery acid in her tea."

Laughing, the three led her away from the Mix Master before her glare became an action she would regret later. The trip to the office was a short one as it lay next door to the library. Since Portia was unable to speak, it fell on Rhys. He too was a legacy student, and not only was his family the biggest contributor to the Academy, but twelve of his older siblings had already graduated. All twelve had gone on directly to management positions, including three in the Recovery Agency, and Rhys would be the only one with field experience. As his grandfather was fond of saying, a Romanov did not get their claws dirty. Suddenly, Rhys was extremely nervous and he swallowed hard into a suddenly dry throat.

The four walked into the main office, where a youngish woman in her twenties sat behind a desk with a high bar surrounding it on two sides. Sayd pushed Rhys forward when he hesitated, causing the woman to look up.

"Can I help you, sweetheart?"

Rhys blushed, turning beet red. Something tumbled from his mouth that sounded like, blah-ba-hum-bah. Or something equally as intelligence. Tongue-tied, the last of Rhys' confidence fled the field foot, horse and artillery.

"Uhm," Lacy said, "we're new students. We just transferred in and we were told to come to the office for our timetables. You know, our classes and stuff."

"What's your name, sweetheart?" The receptionist asked, opening a program on her computer.

"Oh yeah," Lacy giggled. "I'm Lacy Wolfen, this charming gentleman is Rhys Romanov, that's Portia Bishop, and, of course, Sayd Wraith."

"Let's do one at a time," the receptionist smiled. "You're Lacy. Could you spell your last name?"

"Just like it sounds," Lacy grinned. "W-O-L-F-E-N."

One by one, the four received their timetables

and headed out to find their homerooms. Already the first and second bells had rung and they were running late. Both Lacy and Rhys had homerooms on the second floor, while Portia's and Sayd's were here on the first floor. Splitting up, the four paired up and headed toward their class. Lacy and Rhys found his classroom around the first corner, and Lacy found herself roaming the halls alone. The school was big and confusing, and the numbering system did not make sense to her. Lacy never liked being alone, werewolves being a pack culture and very social, but she knew she had a job to do, and concentrated on finding her classroom in the maze of halls she found herself in.

It was off of a hidden hallway that a kindly custodian helped her find. Knocking on the door, the teacher came and opened the door.

"Hi," she said, "I'm Lacy." And then she remembered to hand the teacher the form they had given her in the office.

"Oh, a new student," the teacher smiled a greeting. "Find a seat. Anywhere you like."

Lacy spotted an empty desk at the front of the classroom with a nice comfortable chair. Moving passed the teacher, she made a beeline for this desk and settled in. Her classmates laughed.

"What are you doing?"

"You told me to sit anywhere I like," Lacy said. "And I like this chair. It's very comfortable."

"Yes, it is," the teacher frowned, "that's why it's mine."

"Oh," Lacy gasped. "I'm sorry."

Lacy corralled her bag before it made a break

for it and made her way towards an empty desk at the back of the room. Sitting down, she settled into her seat with a satisfied sigh. "I like this chair. It's very comfortable. At my old school, we all had to sit on a wooden bench, and it was very hard on your bum."

"I'm sure it was," the teacher replied, asking. "And where did you go to school before here?"

"Dante's Academy."

"Hmmm," the teacher mused, "I'm not familiar with that school. Where is it located?"

Lacy panicked, and then she remembered what she was supposed to say if the humans found anything she did strange. "Uhm, Quebec."

Chapter 3

Poltergeists were odd creatures. For one, they were as a breed highly absent-minded – one reason they managed to kill themselves in a world where so few creatures died – and no one was more absent-minded than Sayd. Deep in thought, he forgot where he was or even the mission he was on, a trail of paper flying from the wall in his wake. Lockers spit out their contents, books, papers and binders flying across the hall and into those trying to navigate the mess behind him. Ahead, two boys rough-housing closed the doors that led to the balcony and the main stairs leading down to the atrium. Still lost in thought, Sayd walked through the doors, the tornado of paper, pencils and textbooks slamming into the barrier with a solid thud.

Sayd walked down the stairs, an occasional foot sinking beneath the surface of the step without notice. He missed being alive, of course. Who wouldn't? Not that many people noticed him when he was living, especially with his habit of scuttling off to hide in dark corners, but being a total outcast was far worse. Being dead in the Otherworld was like being a crazy drug addict in this one. People tended to avoid you as much as possible.

With a sigh, he paused at the foot of the steps to look around at his surroundings, a blizzard of paper settling about his feet. He was due to meet the others in the cafeteria, and for the life of him could not remember where it was. Seeing a stream of students moving in through a set of double doors to his right, he set his feet to follow them, his mind still wandering to the problems of the dead.

A whirlwind rose ahead of him, sweeping the food of the nearest table in a tornado of fruit, sandwiches and cooked dishes. Odd bits of food came flying out of the vortex, finding unsuspecting victims seated at the table directly ahead, and the ones to the left. Startled cries of surprise and shock rose as a second and third whirlwind rose at the centre of the room, pelting more students with a slurry of rice and sandwiches. Screams and curses rose, attracting the attention of those in the atrium and the office, bringing a rush towards the door to discover the cause of all the commotion.

Portia glared at Sayd. There was a little more zip in the hex she zapped him with, startling him out of his thoughts.

"What was that for?"

"That!" Portia spun him about to witness the chaos he had caused.

"Oh!"

"Oh is right," Rhys sneered. "You might as well put a billboard up saying 'agents from the otherworld here'."

"Sorry," Sayd mumbled. "I forgot."

"Keep forgetting like that and you're liable to get us all killed," Portia wiped a strand of spaghetti out of her eyes and flicked it towards the poltergeist. "You remember what we learned in history class about all those agents who have gotten caught in the past."

"Sure," Sayd said. "It won't happen again."

Lacy pulled the others into an alcove by the stage as the principal strode into the cafeteria. He took one look at the mess, hands on his hips, and stormed. "Who's responsible for this mess?"

The students turned to stare at the principal, some wiping food from their faces and hair, but otherwise, no one said a word. Hidden in the little alcove that led to the back of the stairs, the four agents waited with bated breaths. Would the principal notice them hiding in here? And if he did, what would happen? There was no way to contact their superiors at the Ministry, nor time for them to arrange an extraction.

"Clean this up!" The Principal snapped. "And I better be able to see my reflection on those tables when you are done."

Lacy peaked around the corner, quickly

ducking back into the alcove. "He's coming!"

Panicked, Sayd ducked through the door, starting up onto the stage when he remembered his companions and turned back. Opening the door, he stood holding it while the others rushed inside.

As he paused, Portia grabbed an ear and led him up the stairs. "Oh no, you don't!"

"What?"

"You were going to stick your head through the door and scare him," Portia said flatly.

"I was only going to take a peak," Sayd complained.

"You and your peaks have got us into enough trouble as it is," Rhys said. "Now, we need to sneak back into the library and our lair."

"I'm all for that," Portia wiped some red liquid and noodles from her hair. "I need to wash this human slop off of me."

"I believe it's called spaghetti," Lacy added helpfully.

"I don't care if it's called goblin food," Portia said, "I need it off of me as soon as possible. It feels so," she shuddered, "gross."

Later, the four gathered in the living room of their lair, three of them freshly showered and redressed. Their uniforms, covered in a collection of goop from the food fight in the cafeteria, were in the washing machine, which busily hummed and churned away as it washed the latest load. Portia turned to the others, saying, "we need to do something about this one. If he forgets one more time we're all apt to end up in the fire, or something worse."

"Someone has got to be with him at all times," Rhys agreed, "but we all have different classes. The Ministry arranged it that way to cover as many of our suspect pool as possible."

"We'll just have to change our schedules," Lacy shrugged.

"Guys," Sayd said, "I'm right here."

"We know you are," Portia snorted. "And that's the reason we are in this mess."

"Uhm," Lacy swallowed. "We have another problem. I forgot my potion. You know, that one that keeps me from transforming."

"I did too," Rhys admitted. "Not to keep me from becoming a werewolf, but the one that keeps me from craving blood."

"Great," Portia rose and began pacing. "Well, I think I might be able to do something with the potions, but what do we do about our schedules?"

"Why don't we do it the same way the Ministry did?" Lacy asked. "They just changed things on the computer thingy."

"Because we aren't experts on human artifacts," Portia said.

"I can do it," Sayd said. "What, it was my hobby."

"You better go with him Rhys," Portia said. "Lacy and I will see if we can find the ingredients for the anti-transmogrification potions. I can't understand how they could have sent any of you out into the field when you can't even keep your minds on the mission."

Sayd pulled Rhys towards the door before he could respond and say something that was bound to start a huge argument. They had enough problems without being at each others' throats. He knew exactly where they needed to go – the guidance offices that were located to the left of the library.

Outside, the library was empty and quiet. Rhys and Sayd nearly jumped out of their skin when the automatic lights came on, freezing them in their tracks. By now, it was eight o'clock in the evening, even the custodians had finished for the day and left the school empty. The sudden appearance of light was enough to stop their heart. Who had lit the tiny torches housed in those glass tubes the humans used to light their homes? Looking around, they could see no one. But if a servant had not gone around and lit the torches, then someone had to have cast a fire spell. And they could see nothing but an empty room and the rows of shelves full of books.

"Must be a ghost," Rhys joked and failed to lighten the mood.

"Let's just get out of here," Sayd said. "The sooner we get this done the sooner we can get back to the lair where things are normal."

The pair left the library, pausing at the door to check that the coast was clear before dashing towards the guidance offices. Here, Rhys waited while Sayd stepped through the door to let him inside, the whole time feeling as if someone was watching him. But that was ridiculous, right, they were alone in the school. Somehow the thought was not as reassuring as it should have been. There was something totally spooky about the human world with its mechanics and science. Better the trusty occult where you knew the results rather than these experiments run amok, and things that did not even have the good graces to greet you when you asked for services.

"Hurry," Sayd urged. "We need to use a computer in one of these offices."

Rhys nodded and followed his friend across the outer office. This was one chore he was happy to leave to the poltergeist. The office lights snapped on by themselves, and once again the two paused to share of shudder. It was as if by some mechanical process they could sense their presence, and that just wasn't natural.

"Wait here," Sayd whispered, "and I'll unlock the door."

Once again he stepped through the door, turning to let Rhys in through the open portal. It was such a hassle to have colleagues who could not just step through a door and had to have it unlocked and opened. It so slowed them down.

"So this is a computer?" Rhys stared down at the apparatus on the desk. "Hello, computer. Could you please call up our class schedules?"

Sayd rolled his eyes as he sat in the chair and pulled it up in front of the computer. "Human things don't work that way. First, you have to infuse it with power like this."

After pushing the power button the screen suddenly lit up. Rhys jumped back, laughing when nothing leapt out to pull him inside. "I wasn't scared. I was just playing you."

"Whatever," Sayd muttered, pecking at the keyboard to unlock the computer. He had accidentally seen the password while looking over the shoulder of the head guidance councillor after sticking his head through the ceiling.

"I thought you said this would only take a second," Rhys complained after Sayd sat staring at the screen for a long spell.

"I'm choosing my courses," Sayd snapped. "Some of the courses you three are taking are boring. "

"Just make sure one of us is in each class and let's get going."

Meanwhile, Portia and Lacy left the lair on their own errand. They decided to try looking for spell ingredients in one of the cooking classes first, something the humans called Hospitality. Without Sayd they would have to rely on Lacy and a werewolf's natural talent for picking locks. Which was probably for the best, Portia thought, because she wasn't sure how one of these human doors would react to an unlocking spell. Probably begin spouting every secret it had heard since the building of the school, and do that at the top of its voice – if it didn't turn into a black hole and send them to the far side of the universe.

Inside, the two made their way towards the back where the ingredients were kept. They opened cupboards, looking at the jars of spices with a puzzled frown. Portia found some well-aged garlic cloves, but nothing else she recognized. Where were the eyes of newt or the toad toes?

"I don't see how humans could cook anything with this stuff," she complained.

"It does give you the creeps, doesn't it," Lacy said, giving a sudden squeal. "Oooh, I found a bottle of time, only they spell it weird. T-H-Y-M-E.”

Portia studied the bottle Lacy handed her and then with a shrug threw it into her bag. “Couldn’t hurt.”

Finding nothing much of interest here, they decided to try the potion rooms up on the second floor. “They do science in those rooms,” Lacy warned. “I have a class in one of them, and I tell you it’s creepy to the max. It raises the hair on my back just thinking about it.”

“Needs must,” Portia hissed back. “Try not to touch anything you don’t recognize and we should be fine.”

A half-hour later, the four met up in the lair. Lacy and the two boys leaned against the counter, watching as Portia worked. She had gathered a variety of spell components, and while none of them were familiar to her, she was sure she could work out some kind of a potion that would keep Rhys from his bloodlust and Lacy from her moon madness. The only problem she was having was that the Mixmaster refused to cooperate.

“Blah!” Mixmaster shouted, hopping about the counter. “You are trying to poison me! What is this terrible stuff you are forcing into me?”

“It says, cinnamon,” Lacy offered. “How bad could it be? It’s brown. Or maybe it's red. Well, it’s brownish red, and that’s the same colour as bat’s wings now isn’t it.”

“Colour and taste have nothing to do with each other,” Mixmaster complained. “Oh, someone, please save me.”

"Don't like your own medicine I see," Rhys teased.

"We'll see who's laughing when it's your turn to taste this noxious potion," Mixmaster snapped.

And with that, Rhys shut up and tried not to pay too much attention to what was going into the Mixmaster. Soon enough he would have to swallow Portia's concoction, and the less he knew about it, the better off he would be. Meanwhile, the Mixmaster screwed up its eyes and set to work mixing the potion with a will. From time to time when something totally disgusting was added, he gave an evil grin and winked at Rhys, who was by now turning an interesting shade of green.

"There," Portia poured the bubbling liquid into a cup, "it's finished. Go ahead, Rhys, drink it down."

"I'm not touching that."

"Oh, don't be a baby," Lacy laughed, picking up the cup and draining it. As she slapped the cup down onto the counter, she hiccupped and her left ear swelled to four times its normal size and became pointed and warty.

The other three broke out laughing.

"What?" Lacy demanded.

"Nothing," Portia choked on her laughter. "Just a slight side effect. I can fix it with a slight adjustment to the potion."

But could she, using only the ingredients she could find in the Human world?

Chapter 4

Abalaxia 47 was no joke at the Academy. A potion that upon consumption would magnify the abilities and powers of supernatural beings, it had been used for centuries by those who practiced the dark arts. These four paranormal students had heard the stories of its use since they were small children. However, traces of Roids 47(formally Abalaxia 47) had been located in Otherworld, the world of the Humans, where their kind often faced persecution and gruesome deaths. When used by humans, the potion was no longer just an enhancement. It was a drug. Much like steroids, it gave humans strength, speed, and endurance. Nevertheless, it also comes with severe side effects following injection. Monstrous side effects.

Quite literally, humans slowly evolve into the utmost bizarre creatures and fiends. This drug had been linked to one of the most stereotypical places to find steroids, a high school. John Paul II Secondary School to be exact. The Academy could not afford to sit back and allow the theft and abuse of this prohibited knowledge. It was dangerous. Yet, someone was supplying it to humans, and those changed by its side effects were finding their way back into the Otherworld. The Academy knew sending their best agents would be too difficult given their age and habits, leaving them unable to blend in without risking the operation. They would appear much older. Youthful agents were needed, graduated or not. Portia, Rhys, Sayd, and Lacy were top in their studies, yet not quite graduated. Each student was capable of blending in with a crop of suspects who were their age, and so the Ministry of Magical Retrieval decided that they were an adequate substitution.

After spending half a school day studying students in their classes and around the school, the group was ready for lunch. They reckoned spending it in the cafeteria would provide them with a better opportunity to remain on task whilst eating.

"I am starvinggg" Rhys groaned.

"Please tell me you're not gonna go fruit ballistic again" Sayd teased.

"No, Brussel boy, but I could really go for some pasta right now" Rhys countered, uncasing his neatly packed dish of tortellini. It was topped with a delicious yet peculiar smelling red sauce. His stomach grumbled. Sayd overlapped his arms in disenchantment but let out a small grin in the crook of his mouth.

The four sat down at a small table in the middle of the cafeteria. They figured staying in the middle would allow each of them to keep sight of different sections of the place. It was quite large and had students scattered in every direction. Fans whirred and students' voices echoed, their conversations merging into a blur of babble. Lacy munched on a bag of chips she had knocked from the vending machine earlier and Portia had a gracefully made sandwich cut diagonally down the center. Sayd appeared to only poke at his food, nudging it around the Tupperware.

After sitting amidst the crowd of multiple cliques, listening to a chaotic slur of inanities, they had overheard a conversation that piqued their interest. The conversation was centred at a table surrounded by jocks from the basketball team, and on one player in particular. He was receiving praise for his impressive performance during morning practice. Someone referred to his skills as otherworldly and nearly impossible to achieve, and it was this combination of words that piqued their interest. Sayd and Portia eyed each other, sure they were onto something, but it still seemed like it wasn't enough information. Just then, the jock sitting a couple of tables in front of them aggressively pushed back in his chair. The scholars turned. The jock had flicked his tongue out like a giant frog and had caught a fly mid-air that was fifteen feet away. His face flushed with a look of shock. Covering his mouth, he ran out of the cafeteria.

"Did you guys see that?" whispered Portia. She leaned into the table.

Nodding their heads aggressively the others responded, "Yeah, we did."

"Yay! Our first monster!" Lacy exclaimed, her high-pitched voice carrying to the nearby tables. She shook her fists in exhilaration.

"You all remember protocol, right?" asked Portia.

"Of course," replied Rhys "Anyone who is exhibiting signs of taking Roids 47 must be kidnapped and given the antidote blah blah blah"

"What he said," Sayd added, pointing this thumb towards Rhys.

"We should divide into teams," proposed Portia. "Sayd and I will follow him while Lacy and Rhys search out a quiet place where we can give him the antidote"

They packed up their lunch and separated themselves into teams. It wasn't long until Rhys and Lacy came upon an empty bathroom that appeared to be under maintenance.

"Do you think that'll work?" Rhys asked.

"It should do," Lacy replied.

They both felt relatively confident that this was the place. How they were going to lure this creature here was all they had to worry about. The monster would be easy to manipulate due to its taste for Otherworld flesh, so they could use themselves as bait. It would be dangerous. Something an untamed amphibious creature would run amok, and the number of humans here could be like a trail of breadcrumbs.

"What about worms?" suggested Rhys "I saw some outside on the pavement this morning"

"Hmm…worms! Oh my God! Gag me with a spoon! That's genius!" Lacy exclaimed, already heading towards one of the back doors of the school. She spun while she walked almost making herself dizzy.

The two of them collected as many worms as they could on the damp pavement and made their way back into the school. Mutually, they decided it would be best to wait outside the bathroom until they were given a signal from Sayd or Portia.

Meanwhile, Sayd and Portia continued to trail behind the jock as it practically slithered down the hallways. Knocking into lockers and clutching its head, the creature wove a path through the throngs of students. From a distance, Portia spotted Lacy pacing around the bathroom door. The two locked eyes as the creature headed in the direction of the unused bathroom. Lacy gave Portia an exaggerated wink before revealing the worms she had kept in her pocket. The worms squirmed in a gross tangle in her hands. She swiftly scattered them among the entrance of the bathroom, making a footpath to the inside. The creature picked up the scent of the worms and darted towards the bathroom where it tumbled through the doorway. Rhys and Lacy stumbled back avoiding the being's grasp. It twirled itself around licking up every single worm within its range. The four students checked their surroundings making sure there were no witnesses as they followed it inside, Rhys shutting the door behind them.

Portia stared down the hideous monster, its eyes now yellow with a small slit of black down the center, its skin laced with lesions. Sayd, Lacy, and Rhys lunged forward, grabbing hold of the creature, sliding it down to the ground, and steadying it for the antidote. It felt unsavoury and almost pitiable.

Portia remained dedicated to their task without thought. "The antidote, now!" she demanded.

She was speaking to her bag, but it refused to give it to her, scuttling into one of the stalls. Similar to a dog playing fetch, it kept just out of reach. Portia aggressively placed out her hand attempting to convince her bag to release the serum. But in doing so, that only made it want to play more. Portia chased her bag everywhere around the bathroom struggling to move around the narrow space between the stalls and the sinks.

"For the love of stars, get back here!" she shouted.

Her voice rasped with frustration. The bag was spitting out hairbrushes with knots tied around the bristles, books, and chewed pencils from its mouth before Portia finally tackled it underneath the hand dryer. The hand dryer had turned on. Its obnoxiously loud humming caused everyone to jolt. She angrily grunted at her mystic bag, beads of sweat dangling off her chin. This wasn't even the battle she came in here for.

"Sometimes I wish I had a normal backpack. You are useless!" Insulted Portia.

Her bag let out a whimpering motion before

releasing the potion.

"Thank you," said Portia, regretting her harsh words.

She grabbed the antidote and threw her bag back onto our shoulder.

"Okay, now where were we?" Portia huffed, rotating herself to see the others losing their grip on the monster.

It burst out of their grasp. The monster had fallen into a fit of rage knocking into one of the sinks and smashing the mirror centred above him. It then began to struggle, ripping soap dispensers straight off the wall, overturning the garbage, and causing all of the toilets to overflow. Nearly slipping on water, the student wrestled around the bathroom to catch this monster. They couldn't let it leave the bathroom.

"Rhys, you're strong. I need you to stay on him with Lacy so we can pin him down to properly deliver the antidote," Portia explained "Sayd, stay guard of the door"

"On it" the three replied in unison.

They scattered themselves around the room, taking up their assigned positions. Sweat was dripping from all their faces and Portia was practically panting. Rhys and Lacy eyed each other trying to be synchronized in their actions.

"On go. Ready?" Rhys asked Lacy.

She nodded.

"1"

"2"

"3"

"Go!" they yelled in harmony.

Lacy kicked the legs of the monster causing it to fall rearward into the backside wall of one of the stalls. The creature choked on its tongue as Rhys slammed his body weight into it, striking it hard against the brick wall. The fluorescent tube lights above them had flickered from the force. Rhys winced. The jock monster had buckled unconscious gurgling in agony. Lacy bit her tongue envisioning how much that had to have hurt.

"You should join the football team" she joked.

"You think?" Rhys questioned.

"Mhm. You just nearly put this thing through the wall" Lacy said, giving him a friendly smile.

He smiled back not knowing how else to respond. It wasn't every day that he heard a sentence like that.

"Will you guys stop chitchatting and move before this thing wakes up?" Portia demanded. She seemed sick of the entire situation at this point. "I don't really feel like chasing it all over the place again. Do you?"

They both shook their heads apologetically and stepped out of the way. They noticed Sayd behind them who grew bored of standing near the door a long time ago. He was fidgeting with shards of the mirror that were hovering in his inattentiveness. Paying no mind to it, Portia stabbed the syringe into a small container filled with the antidote and pulled back the plunger allowing the antidote to make its way into the barrel of the needle. A drip of the serum puddled on the floor as she rid of any air pockets in the needle.

"This might hurt a little," she said, leaning over

the senseless jock. "Can someone please prop his head still for me?"

"Oh, heck yeah! I want in on some of this action." Sayd chirped.

 He crouched down to the sunken body's level analyzing its face.

"Dang this thing is even creepier up close" he babbled, lifting the monster's tongue and waving it around.

"Yeahhh, those eyes are giving me the heebie-jeebies," said Rhys, amplifying some fake chills.

Sayd finally propped the head up, holding it still for Portia. She was working on getting a quick blood sample from the monster's wrist to take for testing. This was their first encounter after all, and she wanted all the information she could get. After putting the vile away in her bag, Portia skillfully began to trace the neck of the jock trying to locate a vein. She was always extremely careful when it came to things like this. When she found one, she scrunched her eyes and exhaled as she inserted to syringe into the vein allowing the antidote to neutralize the intense toxin. The jock's lips quivered in slight pain, but the rest of his body laid still.

"Do you think hc's gonna be okay?" asked Lacy.

"Other than a possible concussion from Rhys, yes. He should be fine." Replied Portia with a comforting tone.

Lacy was visibly stressed, almost huddling herself into a back corner. She toyed with her feet, gaze not parting from the ground.

Sayd, becoming cognitive in the current

situation, watched her with sympathy. "Do you think he'll remember anything?" he asked.

"He shouldn't, given the fact that the monster technically was not him. Plus, he hit his head hard enough not to remember anything that happened all day" she let out a soft chuckle and the others did the same.

The thaumaturgic students took a second to catch their breath. Portia then commenced picking up all the clutter that had been freed from her bag. One of her books was completely soaked with water.

"Yep, this book's a goner." She declared, picking it up by the corner and whipping it into the trash.

It was a sketchbook that she didn't care much for anyway. Lacy then began to pick up some of the trash that was speckled everywhere.

"I guess it's a good thing this bathroom was already under maintenance, huh?" She giggled.

Rhys let out a breathy laugh along with her. They had forgotten to tell the others that it was empty due to maintenance needs.

Sayd crossed his arms. "So, what are we supposed to do about all..." he paused and made a circling motion with his finger around the jock's motionless body "...this?"

"I guess we just leave him here." Said Rhys "we can't have anything blowing our cover."

"But are we sure that's the smartest thing to-," Rhys was cut off.

"He's right" agreed Portia as much as she hated to admit it. "he'll soon wake up and think he spaced out or something."

The others swayed their heads up and down slowly in understanding.

"Right. Then let's get out of here" insisted Rhys.

The students exited the bathroom one by one, checking for any witnesses. They stealthily made their escape down the corridor to the right and walked into a crowd of other students in an attempt to blend in. They halted at the intersection of another hallway. Lacy and Sayd shared an awkward fist bump while the students took an inhalation of their first triumph.

Chapter 5

Sayd, Lacy, Portia, and Rhys drew near the atrium and began to discuss how bizarre the events surrounding their mission were. During their first encounter with Roids 47, they felt like they had run a mile. They needed to plan how to figure out who is distributing this drug, but their mission brief had left them poorly prepared for the situation on the ground. Human students, flesh-eating monsters, and somewhere a shadowy figure or figures feeding poison to the local populace. And on top of all that, they needed to find a way to blend into a world that was so strange and bizarre.

"Okay, so this is a lot more urgent than I thought," said Portia with a slightly frightened tone "We have to get some sort of lead as to who's supplying Abalaxia 47"

"But how? We have no clue what we are looking

for," said Rhys.

"Just look out for anyone who is acting strange or out of place, besides Sayd," said Lacy giggling.

Sayd rolled his eyes, but he couldn't disagree. The four agents from the Ministry of Magic's Retrieval Agency started to wander and pace around the top floor halls before their class started. They were still attempting to become familiar with their surroundings. Continuing back down to the main floor, they headed towards the gym. Portia leaned down to a nearby water fountain and cautiously gathered her hair away from her face as she took a cool sip of water. It felt nice after the game of catch the monster.

Rhys croaked as he propped himself against one of the supports in the hallway. That was until he caught a glimpse of Lacy with giddy eyes and a bouncy stance. The others grew curious as to why she was so excited, turning to look down the hall. Rhys forced himself off the support and brought himself to Lacy's viewpoint. Portia and Sayd followed. Lined across the wall of the gymnasium's foyer was a glass case of trophies, plaques, medallions, and memorabilia. Some of the items had a sparkling gold glare in the light of the hallway. Lacy was entranced.

Sayd caught sight of the look of ecstasy on Lacy's face through the mirroring of the glass. It made him smile. His smile was not vivid, but it was there. Collectively they paced forward to admire the illuminating trophy case. Rhys and Portia leaned against the glass, smudging it with their fingers. Lacy's face was fully pressed against it, her breath causing the glass to fog.

"I want to know why none of our cases ever look this spotless." Portia snickered.

"Probably because they've never had to deal with students like us before," Rhys remarked.
They all chuckled in unison but were cut off by a rough breath down their spines.

The principal had noticed them leaning against the trophy case. He was infatuated with his school's accomplishments and would take a bullet for his prized trophy case. A deep shade of red engulfed his complexion.

"What in the name are you kids doing!?" he roared.

The group shrank in unease and quickly spun to retreat down the hallway. The tall figure of the principal hurtled towards them but instantaneously found himself eyeing the filth coating the glass. Walking over to the case, he bent forward to inspect the prints with utter disgust. Loosening his striped tie, he began to polish their smudged fingerprints and Lacy's face marks. Sayd, being the phantom he was, had nothing to worry about. Still pacing themselves away from the gymnasium, the four had come to a halt after hearing some nearby students humorously laughing at them.

"What's so funny?" Portia asks them.

"Don't you know not to touch the trophy case?! The principal treats them like his pride and joy, and he will do anything to keep them safe and win more." The other kids responded, speaking all at once. "Yeah, like they were his children or something. You're all so dead. Probably get expelled."

"O.M.G we like...totes forgot" Lacy interrupted, attempting to dim any suspicions. She side-eyed her new friends as if she was searching for their approval. However, the others were too fixated on their peer's reactions. Rhys gave a self-conscious grin echoed by the others as they continued down the hall.

They all let out a shared exhale as they gathered in a huddle.

"Did you guys also catch what they said?" Portia asked, raising her eyebrows.

"That the principal is crazy? Yeah, I gathered that." Rhys declared.

"I'm pretty sure she's referring to his obsession with winning," said Sayd.

"Yeah, didn't they say he would do anything if it meant winning more trophies?" Lacy jumped in.

"Correct," Portia replied "it may be a bit a stretch, but I think we should mark him down as our first suspect. I mean- he definitely seems to have the drive to achieve what we're searching for, right?"

"Agreed."

"Agreed."

Portia whipped her bag around her shoulder to face her and retrieved a notebook and pen from the front pouch. She flipped the cover over and quickly scribbled:

First Suspect: Principal- will do anything to have his students win.

Just then, the warning bell for class rang and Lacy and Sayd directed themselves upstairs towards their class on the second floor. As they are walking, they pass the chapel. Sayd noticed that the doors were padlocked. However, they were slightly open. Lacy traced his gaze and found herself beaming with curiosity. She tiptoed over to the oversized doors and obviously had to glimpse through the fracture in the doors. Before she could get a proper look, Sayd decided that instead of looking through the crack, he could easily put his head through the door. He would also be able to cover more surface area of vision this way. Lacy nodded in agreement but continued to look through the slightly ajar door. She wanted to see for herself as well. The two witness the chaplain closing the lid of a small box and locking something inside. The chaplain began to turn around as if she knew they were there. Lacy grabbed Sayd by the collar and pulled him back through the door. They continued down the hallway in fear that she'd come looking.

"I wonder what she's hiding in that box," Lacy whispered with a suspicious attitude.

"You don't think the creator of the world would be giving Roids 47 to students, do you?" Sayd asked.

'The creator of the world'?" Lacy replied, confused by what he was getting at.

"Yeah, that lady that was in there," said Sayd, growing unconfident of what he was saying "I read about it before we came here. Humans believe this person created everything in this world."

"That's the chaplain not the 'creator of the world'," Lacy giggled. "Although, you're not wrong. They do believe in a creator of this world. They call it 'God', but it is definitely not that woman in there. She's far too wrinkly"

They both laughed as they finally made their way to class.

Since the beginning of the day, Rhys had noticed that the science teacher always locked himself away in his classroom whenever he walked by. During fifth period, he spotted the teacher desperately lowering the blinds draped on the back of the classroom door. He tried to enter but the door wouldn't budge. Putting his ear up to the door, he heard something clang and would have continued to investigate but was driven away by a putrid smell coming from the room.

"Bleh- smells like garlic." He gagged to himself.

The four students all made their way to their lair to discuss all the new information and discoveries they had made. Rhys was about to share what he had just witnessed when he was interrupted. The Mixmaster 2000 announced that it will be making a delicious and special treat for concluding their day of hard work and progress. They all tilted their heads as they made eye contact with each other.

"Drinks all around, I guess then!" Portia exclaimed, making a face at her companions. Who knew what the crazy machine would come up with today?

They watched as the machine began to make this so-called 'special treat', but something wasn't right. Smoke began roiling out from beneath its lid, and a chugging filled the kitchen that was interspersed by a definite cough.

"Is it just me or is the Mixmaster much louder

than normal?" Lacy said, raising her voice over the sound.

"It doesn't sound rig-" Rhys begins to say when he was interrupted once again by the Mixmaster making a gagging noise.

It then began to overflow like a washing machine with too much soap. Soon, the lair was filled with seafoam and toadstool soup. The group swam against the current, where Sayd managed to pull the plug on the runaway machine. Angrily they began to clean up the mess as they discuss what they discovered today.

"The principal seems like he's the dealer," Portia said while mopping around their main table.

"Not necessarily," Sayd retorted. "Lacy and I witnessed the chaplain-" he paused. "It's called a chaplain, right?"

Lacy nodded and continued the story. "We saw her locking something up in the chapel"

"I also saw the science teacher acting very suspicious," Rhys said, picking a piece of toadstool off the ceiling. "He locks himself in his classroom all the time. Not to mention, it also reeks in there"

"How do we know which one it is then?" Lacy questioned.

"We are just going to have to keep an eye on all of them, I guess" Portia replied.

She hated how unsure she sounded. Taking out her notebook once again she scribbled in:

Second Suspect: Chaplain- suspiciously locking things up?

Third Suspect: Science Teacher- locks himself in classroom, odd smell?

They finally finished cleaning up the mess, disappointed that they never got to try the Mixmaster 2000's treat.

"So, I guess I will see you all tomorrow?" Sayd asked, looking desperate to leave.

"Yes, I suppose we should all head to bed, we have classes in the morning," said Portia, packing her things.

"Have a good night, everyone!" Lacy shouted, skipping her way to her room and waving behind her.

Chapter 6

Portia groaned as she plodded up to her locker. She did not understand why they were forced to take English classes when everyone already spoke English. Unfortunately, they did, and it was one of the classes she was assigned. And now she had to write a fifty-thousand-page assignment on the first five chapters of this totally fictional and unbelievable story they were reading in class. Taking her books from her locker and stuffing them into her bag, Portia thought they could have set up their lair here, which would save her from fighting with her bag to get her books back at the end of each day. Unfortunately, the lockers lined the hallways and were far too open to hide their comings and goings from their lair. So the library was the best choice after all.

Still muttering curses directed at her English teacher she slumped down the hall towards the library. If it did not take too long to get her books back from her bag, she might make a start at the assignment before the others showed up to work on their real mission.

The library had its usual scattering of students at this time of day, mostly sitting around tables alone or in small groups of one or two. One table, however, had seven or eight students talking to the security guard. The ambiguity caught Portia's eye as she slipped behind the bulletin board that led to their lair, and she paused to listen.

"Why don't we write a story about three or four students who come from, say, like the Otherworld?" Tara suggested. "Like one could be a witch."

"Oh," Elliot threw in, "one could be a ghost."

"Yeah, and like a werewolf and vampire," Ranah added.

"That sounds interesting," the security guard nodded. "And they could be here to find out who is selling supernatural steroids or something."

Their words froze Portia's blood. Their mission had been compromised. She could not force herself to move into the lair and stood rooted to the spot, listening.

"Where would it be set?" Ben asked.

"At John Paul II," Allan, the security guard answered. "Same as all our books."

"You know," Ben said. "Steroids have side effects. Maybe supernatural steroids, let's call them Abalaxia 47, would slowly turn humans who take them into monsters."

"Yeah," Carly nodded, "like all kinds of weird

monsters. Like frog-like men and blob monsters and stuff."

Portia shook off her shock and dove through the door of the lair. There was no doubt about it, their mission had been discovered. Panicked, she raced to the recall alarm that would send the others back to the lair, but they were already there, gathered around the Mixmaster 2000 as it worked on some afterschool smoothies. Panting, she scrambled into their midst, trying to make herself understood.

"Emergency," she breathed. "Danger. We've been discovered."

"Slow down," Lacy laughed. "I can hardly understand a word you are saying."

"The humans know we are here!"

"How?" Rhys demanded.

"I don't know!" Portia exclaimed. "There is a group of students talking to the security guard even as we speak. They are unravelling our entire mission, telling him everything. They know there is a witch, a vampire, a werewolf – even a ghost. They know all about Abalaxia 47 and its side effects, and even why we were sent here."

"Oh, my Aunt Esmeralda!" Lacy exclaimed. "What are we going to do?"

"We should return home right away," Sayd suggested. "The Great Druid knows what these humans will do to us if they catch us."

"Maybe they will pull our eyes out and use them as garter belts," Lacy shivered. "My grandpa always said that humans do things like that, and I for one am rather attached to my eyes."

"We can't go home with our tail between our

legs," Rhys said. "We'd be the laughingstock of the Ministry – not to mention never being assigned to the Retrieval Agency, maybe even kicked out of the Academy."

"He's right," Portia said, calming herself down. "We can't run home. We'll have to do something about these busybodies."

"Like what?"

"We'll need to trap them," Portia decided. "We have extra traps. We'll just have to use one and hope we won't need it later."

The four fell silent, thinking about the prospect of using a human trap for the first time in the field. The traps, which held the victims suspended in time and space between the two worlds, were famously finicky. And dangerous. One misstep and you could end up caught in the trap instead of your intended prey. And if these humans knew of their mission, they might have a few traps of their own prepared.

"Well," Rhys said, "we can't very well jump them in the middle of a crowded library."

"Sayd," Portia suggested. "Creep out and check things. The ones we want are the only large group, and they are sitting at the table with the security guard. The one that looks like that creature from the horror movies – what's his name – Santa Claus."

Sayd gave her a dirty look. Send the ghost, he muttered, where the living feared to tread. Like we don't matter, or something. Sighing, he gathered himself up and headed towards the door, his battery acid and pine sap smoothy forgotten. With a great gulp of air, he stepped out of the lair head first, taking a look around the area behind the bulletin board to make sure the coast was clear. Satisfied, he poked his head through the bulletin board itself. Noticing that the room was empty except for the one table, where a group of students continued to tell the security guard everything they knew about his companions and his mission.

"What do you think about the name Portia for the witch?" Allan asked. "Does that sound right?"

"Oh, I love it," Tara said.

"It's so Shakespearean," Karlee replied.

Oh my Aunt Esmeralda, Sayd thought, they even know our names. Poking his head back through the bulletin board, he stepped through the door to the lair and back into the anxious group waiting in the kitchen.

"They know everything!" He exclaimed. "They even know our names!"

"We know that," Rhys snapped. "How many people are in the library?"

"It's only them right now," Sayd said. "But we got to act fast before those spies can tell the security guard any more about our mission."

"Okay, let's go!" Portia rushed towards the door.

"Wait!" Lacy complained. "We can't just rush out at them. We need to sneak up on them or something."

"How about if Sayd moves out and shuts down the lights," Rhys suggested. "Lacy, you go and lock the doors while Portia and I move in from the right and the left. How does that sound?"

"Sounds like a plan," Portia said. "Now let's get moving before they get away and spread the alarm."

Nodding, the four took a tighter grip on their supplies and moved as one towards the door of their lair. Pausing, they waited while Sayd once again slipped through the door and outside. Here, he gathered his metaphysical and arcane forces and released a wind that swept through the library, rattling the windows, knocking books off the shelves, and finally taking out the lights. When the lights went out the other three leapt out of the lair. Lacy raced towards the doors with a length of chain, quickly wrapping it around the two handles and locking the two doors together so they could not be opened from either inside or out. Next Portia and Rhys ran to either side of the table, trapping the students and security guard at the table.

"Hey!" Ben cried. "What's going on?"

"Now!" Rhys shouted.

Portia removed a crystal orb from the pocket of her cloak. Holding it above her head, she began chanting, releasing the magical powers within the orb and opening a trap from which there was no escape. Allan, the security guard, was halfway to his feet when he was sucked up by a vortex of power. Pulled inside the orb in a long, elastic streak, he disappeared with the others close behind him.

"We got them!" Portia exclaimed.

"Yeah, but look at the mess we made," Lacy said as the lights came up on the wreck of the library, books and papers scattered from one end to the other, chairs and tables knocked over, and computer equipment bunched in a knot at the centre of the room.

"We better clean this up quickly," Rhys said, "before anyone comes and discovers all this. We don't want any questions."

Reluctantly, the four began to put right the library. While Rhys and Sayd put the chairs and tables back in place, and Lacy sat amongst the computer equipment untangling a skein of wires, Portia began hunting down the books and placing them back on their shelves. Some of them were easy to replace, having merely fallen out of place when the shelf they were on was knocked over, but some had been scattered clear across the room. These she had to rely on the magical symbols on their spines, a codex she was not familiar with, and was having some difficulty decoding. She was still working on the books when the others finished their chores and came over to help her.

"You can't just put them higgly-piggly onto any shelf," Portia complained. "They go back in a certain order."

"Does it really matter?" Rhys asked. "Right now we need to put them back onto the shelves as quickly as possible. Let the humans figure this out in the morning. We have work to do, and that means returning to our lair before someone comes along."

Reluctantly, Portia agreed. As long as the books were off the floor, no one would notice their presence until much later. And even then, they would not know what had happened, who had done it, and how the books had become scattered throughout the shelves out of order.

When their work was done the four crept back into their lair, exhausted. Too exhausted to object when the Mixmaster offered to make them a sour lemon pucker, a drink so sour it could purse your lips for a week. Sitting around the kitchen as they waited, Lacy picked up the orb and gave it a shake, staring at the tiny figures inside.

Tara brushed lint from the sleeve of her security guard uniform.

"Why don't we write a story about three or four students who come from, say, like the Otherworld?" Allan suggested. "Like one could be a witch."

"Oh," Jacob threw in, "one could be a ghost."

"Yeah, and like a werewolf and vampire," Ben added.

"That sounds interesting," the security guard nodded. "And they could be here to find out who is selling supernatural steroids or something."

"Where would it be set?" Ben asked.

"At John Paul II," Tara, the security guard answered. "Same as all our books."

"You know," Carly said. "Steroids have side effects. Maybe supernatural steroids, let's call them Abalaxia 47, would slowly turn humans who take them into monsters."

"Yeah," Adrienne nodded, "like all kinds of weird monsters. Like frog-like men and blob monsters and stuff."

Lacy frowned and gave the orb a hard shake. She could almost make out what the tiny figures were doing inside if she squinted in the right way.

The werewolf picked up the mug of sour lemon puck Rhys set down in front of her and gave the orb another shake.

Ranah fixed the collar of her uniform shirt and looked out at the other members of the Pens of John Paul II. "Is anyone else feeling dizzy?"

Chapter 7

Sayd was chafing at the constraints of his companions. How was he to find out anything if every time he gave in to his curiosity one of them pulled him back? Portia alone must have zapped him at least a dozen times in their Math class. It wasn't his fault that he slipped so easily through these human chairs. And Rhys wasn't any better, always hissing at him with those perfect fangs. Sayd had half a mind to slime his bed but Sayd wasn't sure the vampire would notice since he slept in a coffin every night.

So it was little wonder that when it was Lacy's turn to mind him that Sayd gave her the slip. Telling her that he was going to his room to chill, Sayd slipped out the back. Not that the lair had a back door, but when you were a poltergeist the lack of a door didn't matter much.

"Funny," Sayd thought, "I didn't know that this was here."

He was in some kind of office belonging to one of the humans. Since he was already here, Sayd decided he might as well explore. There was nothing like poking into someone else's drawers, rummaging through their stuff and wondering what it was and why they had kept it. And if you could drive them a little batty by moving their things about, well that only added icing to the cake, so to speak.

Sayd had just settled in for a good rummage when he heard footsteps approaching. Had Lacy found him already? Quickly he ducked through the nearest wall. He found himself in the IT room, which, being full of his favourite human artifacts, was far more promising. Sticking his head through the screen of a monitor, he wondered if he could get one of the units going and whether any of the humans would notice if he borrowed one. He always did want to search for the ghost in the machine, having so many questions to ask that being, although, without a machine, his search was doomed to fail.

That prospect held his attention for a good ten minutes. Bored, he drifted out into the hall and down towards the gym. School was out and the halls were rapidly emptying. Only a few afterschool programs were running, mostly athletics, so all the action was at this end of the school. And if Sayd was anything, he was a man of action.

"Oh no, you don't, girl!"

"Ha!" A laughing voice retorted. "Who's going to stop me?"

A loud snap and a squeal were more than a poor poltergeist could stand. Sayd stuck his head through the wall and peeked inside.

"Ah! You perv!" A girl screamed.

"Get out of here!"

A hail of shoes came tumbling at him, bouncing off his hand. Sayd pulled his head back through the wall, thinking, "well! They were a screamy lot. And they were hardly naked."

The volume issuing from the change room had increased tenfold, and Sayd decided elsewhere would be a better place to be. He decided that the shortest route was the safest, and so he cut through the wall into the nearest classroom. Continuing towards the atrium through the walls, he left the noise behind.

"What's that?" Sayd wondered as a strangely familiar odour hit his nostrils.

Following the smell, Sayd drifted across the atrium and into the far hallway. The odour was definitely coming from one of the cooking classes. Unlike back in the Otherworld, where they brewed potions in similar classrooms, the humans actually made food. Sayd wondered what human food tasted like and decided he would go find out. Poltergeists had notoriously short memories, and it was a similar curiosity that had led to his death, although now that was long forgotten and only the curiosity remained.

He tracked the aroma to the second cooking class, the one that was closest to the tech hallway.

The class had dispersed for the day but a pot that the teacher had not yet dealt with still stood on the stove. Sayd paused directly inside the door, checking that the coast was clear. His timing was impeccable. There wasn't a screaming girl in sight, and no one else. Feeling confident, he strode to the back of the classroom and lifted the lid from the pot.

"Ah! Aunt Brumhilda's wrinkled knees!" Sayd screamed louder than the girls. "They're trying to poison me!"

Still screaming, Sayd passed the cooking teacher in the doorway, who said, "take it easy, man. They're only Brussel sprouts. It's not like they will kill you."

Having survived his deadly encounter with the Brussel sprouts, his kryptonite and the thing that had killed him, Sayd decided he needed a safe place to calm down. His search brought him to the space behind the stage, where he found an overstuffed chair and collapsed. Who knew the Human world contained those nasty green critters that lurked on your plate waiting to kill? He wasn't the only member of his family to succumb to the dreaded Brussel sprouts. He had an uncle who drowned in a pot of brussel sprout soup, and his Great Aunt Greta had died in an avalanche of green when a truck hauling Brussel sprouts overturned.

Sayd's ruminations were interrupted by the decided sound of whispering voices. The poltergeist sank into the chair to listen.

"Don't worry about it," the first voice husked. "Yes, she looks bad now, but once she gets the full treatment she will be back to normal without anyone being the wiser."

The words sent Sayd scuttling forward. From his new vantage point, he could see two shadowy figures facing each other. Off to one side was a cage similar to that one might see at the circus, and inside something moved. Something green and warty and hairy with too many arms and legs. Face it, if that was a she, she was definitely having a bad hair day.

"Look," the other shadow whispered, "when this all started you assured me the students would come to no harm. Now look at her!"

"You had to know all steroids have minor side effects," the first soothed. "You can't make an omelet without breaking a few eggs."

"You call that minor?" The second shadow seethed. "She shot a slime ball so large it swallowed one of the bleachers. It will take the custodians a week to clean it up."

"Calm yourself," his opposite continued. "This is nothing we can't fix. Besides, you did want to win – what was it again?"

"The girls' basketball championship."

"And you will," the first shadow said. "One more trophy to add to your collection. In the meantime, we will take this poor unfortunate back to our lab for treatment. A few shots, a few days' rest and she will be as good as new without a single memory of what has happened to her."

"I still don't like it," the second muttered. "How am I going to explain her absence?"

"Tell everyone she's in one of those detention

thingies."

"Those only last for fifteen minutes," the second shadow snorted. "And they go home at the end of the day."

"Then tell them she's off to basketball camp to meet with some talent scouts."

"Yes, I think I can make that work. But one more little side effect like this and our deal's off!"

Stunned, Sayd backed into the shadows and sank through the floor into the cupboards beneath the stage. No one was going to believe what he had seen and heard. Someone in the school was using Abalaxia 47 to enhance the performance of the student-athletes. Now all they had to do is figure out the who and the why, and they had this mission all but wrapped up.

Forgetting about slipping away from Lacy, and any of his recent misadventures as poltergeists tended to do, Sayd headed straight back to the lair. He could not wait to tell the others his news. Hopefully, they would believe him, and they could stake out the area until the two men met again.

Coming through the door to the lair, Sayd was greeted by a cry. "Where have you been?"

"Out for a walk."

"Yes," Portia snapped. "We heard."

"Yeah, but I discovered something important."

"Where was it?" Lacy accused. "In the girls' changeroom, or the cooking class?"

"That was just an accident," Sayd stammered, "but -."

"But what?" Rhys demanded. "Are you trying to get our mission scrubbed?"

"No," Sayd wailed, "but if you will just listen."

"Us listen," Portia snorted. "Why should we listen to you when you never listen to us. I don't know why we don't send word back to the Academy and have you sent home."

"Won't anyone listen to me?"

As one, the others turned and left the room, heading into the girls' room where Sayd could not follow.

"Shall I make you a nice cup of hot battery acid and you can tell me all about it?" The Mixmaster asked hopefully.

"Might as well," Sayd sighed. "No one else seems interested in the breakthrough I made in the case."

Humming happily to itself, the Mixmaster busily worked away at a nice hot drink to cheer up one of its masters. From time to time he peeked over to make sure Sayd was still there and still aware of how hard the machine was working. Now it was time to let a little steam escape from the top of its lid – a mere spurt or two lest someone think he had sprung a leak and needed repair. And finally the piece de resistance. With one long squirt, he filled a mug.

"There you go," the Mixmaster said. "Now tell me all about your big discovery."

"You know, I saw the guy who's selling the steroids," Sayd raised his cup and slammed it back down.

"Ah-ha and how is your drink?"

"And I heard their whole plot." Again Sayd raised his mug, "only those three snobs won't stop and listen."

"And the drink?" The Mixmaster asked anxiously. "You don't want it to get cold."

"Oh!" Sayd exclaimed. "And I saw this human in a cage, only it wasn't human anymore, it was a monster. And the one who is selling the Abalaxia 47 is bringing it back to the Otherworld. What do you think that's all about?"

"I wouldn't know," the Mixmaster shrugged. "Your drink?"

"Oh, yeah." Sayd took a sip and spat it out. "Brussel sprout juice. You're all trying to kill me."

"I couldn't get battery acid and so I made a slight substitution."

Chapter 8

The Mixmaster sat churning on the counter. He was choked. No one understood how difficult it was to mix drinks hot and cold, everything from teas to smoothies. Especially in this weird world where honest ingredients, like swamp water and toadstools, had to be substituted for things like sugar and chocolate. And to spit out a drink the Mixmaster had worked so hard preparing, and claiming he was trying to poison them. Nope, that was intolerable.

"There's only one thing for it," the Mixmaster declared. "I shall run away."

"Where shall you go, go?" The grandfather clock intoned.

"I don't know," the Mixmaster admitted, "but somewhere out there is a place where my talents will be appreciated."

Jumping off the counter, he tootled across the room and out the door of the lair without a backwards glance. The world beyond was a lot bigger than he had imagined, and almost he turned back.

"No, I shall not lose my resolve," the Mixmaster squared his shoulders. "My destiny lies this way. Or maybe it's this way."

Making his way out of the library and into the atrium, he paused to assess his surroundings. A lot of traffic seemed to flow through the office on his right, so the Mixmaster decided to check it out. Lost amongst a sea of sneakers, he hopped and wobbled his way towards the door.

"Excuse me," he hopped between a pair of trousered legs. "So sorry about the new kicks, a little alligator saliva never hurt anyone."

With a few more wobbles and hops, the Mixmaster found his way through the door. Once in the office, he paused to look around. Over to his left, he spotted a plant, and beyond this a watercooler. If anyone would know a good spot for a drink mixer to settle, it would be the water cooler. It heard all the latest gossip and knew the comings and going of the entire staff. Here was someone whose acquaintance the Mixmaster needed to make.

Hobbling around the corner, the Mixmaster hopped up onto a shelf beside the watercooler. "I say," it greeted. "This is a busy spot."

Having complimented the watercooler on its choice of locations, the Mixmaster waited patiently for it to return his greeting. After all, protocols had to be observed in these delicate matters. A moment later, a loud bubbling gurgle rose from the water cooler.

"I say," the Mixmaster sniffed. "How rude."

Another gurgling snork rose from the water cooler.

"Are you looking to throw down?" The Mixmaster demanded. "Because I'll have you know I have a black belt in the culinary arts. I can mince and Juliette with the best of them."

Gurgle. Blurp.

"That's it! Engard! Take this! And that! And some more of this!"

His last strike knocked the bottle off the water cooler, sending the liquid inside spilling all over the rug.

"Ha-ha!" The Mixmaster said. "I knocked your block off with one blow. And now, just to teach you a lesson in manners, I'm going to take over your spot and see how you like it to be ignored."

When someone came over for a drink of water, the Mixmaster, still full of himself after vanquishing the watercooler, refused to acknowledge them.

"Hey Mable," the thirsty staff member called, "you better call a custodian. Someone's knocked over the watercooler."

A few minutes later, the old custodian came into the office with a shop vacuum. As he righted the watercooler, he noticed the Mixmaster. "What is this doing here? I better put it away before it gets broken."

With a large hand over its mouth, the Mixmaster was unable to complain as it was carried inside the meeting room and put inside a cupboard. Alone in the dark, the Mixmaster almost exploded with indignation.

"Well, I never! If this is how they treat their appliances, I am off to find a better position. Somewhere in this school is a place where thirsty people will appreciate a drink dispenser like myself."

The Mixmaster hopped out of the cupboard. At the door, it waited patiently for the custodian and the smiling idiot of a vacuum cleaner to finish up. As soon as the coast was clear, the Mixmaster slipped out of the meeting room and out of the office.

Once again in the atrium, it scouted around for a location. A pair of women slipped into an office to the left of the library.

"I've never noticed that before," the Mixmaster muttered. "I think I'll give it a look. Couldn't hurt, after all."

With the same wobbling gait, the Mixmaster made its way across the atrium and slipped into the guidance office. Inside, he jumped up onto the counter of the receptionist's desk and settled in beside a potted plant.

"Do you mind if I sit here a spell?" The Mixmaster asked.

The potted plant nodded in the wake of a passing human.

"Very hospitable of you," the Mixmaster said. "I'm having a tough day. You see, I had to give up my position this morning."

The plant nodded sympathetically in the breeze

of a passing student.

"You see, I wasn't appreciated at my old place," the Mixmaster continued. "Always complaining, never any appreciation of the difficulty in preparing drinks and food on demand."

One of the guidance councillors noticed the Mixmaster on the shelf. "Oh, we got a Keurig machine. I think I'll make myself a coffee."

She returned a moment later with a mug and a coffee pod. Placing the mug on the service tray, she opened the Mixmaster's lid and shoved the pod inside. Suddenly, the Mixmaster's body was infused with the most awful-tasting, foul liquid known to any world. "I'm being poisoned," it thought, unable to scream while choking on the vile substance. Steam began to shoot out every port, whistles and beeps filling the air as the Mixmaster began rocking violently.

"Oh dear," the guidance councillor said, "there's something wrong with this machine."

"We better get some paper towels," the receptionist suggested, leading the way out of the office.

And with that, the Mixmaster made his escape. Panicked, lest his two torturers return, he ran blindly straight into the cafeteria. Here, it took the opportunity to spit out the vile human concoction from its inners while looking for a new home. Apparently, it would be a lot harder than he had thought, but his creator did not raise it to quit at the first hardship. The Mixmaster would search until it found the perfect place. And an opportunity soon presented itself.

The Mixmaster noticed students moving in and out of the two doors on the far side of the cafeteria. Anywhere there was a crowd was a place the Mixmaster wanted to explore. Satisfied its self-cleaning routine had rid it of the last of the vile poison, the Mixmaster tottled over towards the doors and his future.

"This is more like it," the Mixmaster said as he noticed the food in the warming trays and the row of drink dispensers.

Meanwhile, the four agents had returned to the lair to exchange books for their next class. Sayd, thirsty after gym class, went into the kitchen for a drink. "Hey, where's the Mixmaster?"

"What do you mean, where's the Mixmaster?" Rhys demanded. "It's on the counter, right where it always is."

"Well," Sayd said, "it's not here now."

"The Mixmaster is missing?" Portia sighed. "Where could it be?"

"I promised not to tell you that the Mixmaster has run away," the grandfather clock tolled solemnly.

"The Mixmaster has run away!"

"Ah," the clock squawled. "She has discerned the truth with her arcane powers. It just goes to show you that you can't fool a witch."

"This is a disaster," Lacy said. "What do we do now?"

"We're going to have to split up and search the school," Portia said. "Sayd and Rhys go search the office, we'll check guidance. If you don't find it, meet back in the atrium."

"And hurry," Rhys urged, "before it's discovered."

"How?" Lacy asked and answered. "Oh yeah, human things don't talk."

Ten minutes later, the four met up in the atrium. They had lingered in both offices, peering into each room and nosing about without success. If the Mixmaster was ever in either office, it was not there now.

"Where to now?" Rhys asked.

"This is ridiculous," Sayd said. "Doing it your way will take us forever. Stay here and I will find it."

A strong wind suddenly blew through the school, slamming doors and lockers, scattering papers and rattling windows. As quickly as it had risen, it fell away and Sayd stood amongst them again.

"You won't believe where it is," Sayd said. "The Mixmaster is in the cafeteria and there is a large lineup to get in."

"Great," Rhys sighed. "Now what?"

"We could go in and pretend we are placing an 'out of order' sign on it," Lacy suggested.

"Good idea," Portia said. "Sayd, you let us in once Lacy and I make the 'out of order' sign. Once you do, wait outside with Rhys to make sure the coast is clear."

The two girls quickly ripped out a page from a binder and wrote 'out of order' on it. Once they were done, Sayd went ahead and melted through the wall, getting to the door ahead of the girls.

"Hey!" Someone shouted. "No cutting in line."

"We're not," Lacy retorted. "We're putting a

sign on one of the drink machines. It's spitting drinks all over the floor."

Inside, the two girls headed straight for the drink dispensers, where the Mixmaster had made room for itself by pushing one to the back of the counter.

"Oh no, you don't!" The Mixmaster scolded as Portia tried to tape the sign on it. "Just because I am out of warranty doesn't mean I'm broken."

"You need to come back to the lair right now," Portia hissed, "before you compromise our mission."

"I'm perfectly fine right here with my two chums," the Mixmaster sniffed. "Besides, I have an excellent disguise."

"Oh yeah," Portia said, "well human machines don't move on their own and they don't talk."

"Of course they do," the Mixmaster retorted. "Not half an hour ago I had a lovely conversation with a fern."

"Oh yeah, what did it say?"

"Well, it said -," the Mixmaster paused. "Well, it did nod very sympathetically when told how cruelly you have treated me."

"But if you don't come back," Lacy wheedled, "who will fix me my hemlock toddy? You know I can't sleep unless I have a hemlock toddy."

"For you, Miss Lacy," the Mixmaster said with dignity, "I will return to my former position and endure abuse from all quarters."

And as it jumped from the counter Portia caught it and stuffed the Mixmaster in her bag. As one, the two girls turned and made their escape.

Chapter 9

A bent figure stooped over a pot of bubbling liquid, staring down at its surface as one hand stroked his long chin. Vague figures danced in the swirls of the liquid. Lurid dancers stretched and misshapen by the bubbles that brewed beneath the story, they danced a macabre ballet before his eyes, soaking up every drop of his attention.

"Master," a misshapen creature called, dragging a clubbed foot behind her as she moved into the room.

For a moment a stooped figure did not answer. Frowning down at the surface of the green liquid, he straightened. "What is it, Clodagh?"

"There were not as many monsters in this shipment, master," Clodagh whined. "Something is interfering with your plans."

"How many was the shipment short?"

"One or two, master." Clodagh shrugged.

"Well," her master straightened until he was towering over her. "Was it one, or two?"

"One, I think master," Clodagh decided, shaking her shaggy head.

"I will definitely have to look into this," the sorcerer decided. "Fetch me the scrying crystal. And Clodagh, be careful with it. Another crack in my crystal and I will put a crack in your skull."

"Yes, master."

Clodagh moved across the room to a small brassbound chest. With shaky hands, she lifted the lid and raised a cloth-wrapped object from inside. Covered in black silk with stars and other arcane symbols embroidered on its surface, the crystal ball lay protected from dust and dirt and from stray energies that might interfere with its delicate tuning. Holding it with both hands, Clodagh walked back towards her master with delicate, careful steps, not daring to raise her feet off the ground lest she trips with her delicate burden. With a sigh of relief, she set it carefully on the wooden base near her master's right elbow.

"Here it is, Master."

The sorcerer turned, his elbow upsetting the crystal ball and its base. For a moment it wobbled back and forth, Clodagh reaching out to catch it before it fell.

"Now look what you have done!" The sorcerer snapped. "If you have messed up its harmonics, I will feed you to my pets."

"Look, Master!" Clodagh pleaded. "It is perfectly fine. I caught it before it could fall."

Muttering darkly, the sorcerer pushed her aside and took up position behind the crystal ball. Holding his hands over its surface, he watched as purple and blue bolts of static electricity rose from the crystal ball, studying their patterns rising from the heart of the crystal.

"Ah-ha," he said, "what do we have here? Is that the Witch's daughter I see? Now, what is she doing in the Human world?"

"Interfering with your plans," Clodagh guessed.

"Yes, yes, I know that." The sorcerer snapped.

Still studying the crystal, he moved his hands from side to side, steering the point of view along the hallways of John Paul II Secondary School. He focused in on a girl, frowning. "A Lycanthrope. Who is that?"

"That would be High Minister Wulfsblood's granddaughter," Clodagh offered helpfully. "She is the first of her kind to be accepted into the Academy."

"Yes, they will let anyone in these days." His own rejection by the prestigious Academy still rankled, but it was of little matter compared to the plans he had in motion. Soon he would have the power to cow even the Ministry of Magical Artifacts, so what did a piddling little academy matter in the scheme of things.

Readjusting the view, the sorcerer continued to study the students that filled the hallways of the high school. He came across an interesting character and panned back to focus in on a tall, skinny individual with pale skin, and black bags beneath his eyes. "What is this?"

"He looks like a poltergeist, Master," Clodagh nodded excitedly. "Isn't he the one who choked on the Brussel Sprout?"

"Did he?" The sorcerer smiled, a sad, wicked little thing that hardly dented his thin lips. "Are any of our Fungal monsters ready to harvest?"

"One, Master," Clodagh said. "The one you were saving for the inspector from the Ministry of Magical Inquiries."

"No matter," the sorcerer waved away her words. "We have better uses for that creature at the moment. But how to get it to the Human world without alerting anyone?"

"A spell," Clodagh suggested brightly.

"Of course a spell, you moron. You are the worst sorcerer's assistant in either world. Am I not a sorcerer? What else would I do but use my magic?"

The sorcerer fell to thinking, tapping a finger against his long, crooked nose.

"You could mail it," Clodagh offered, deciding he was still waiting for her to answer his question.

"And how would I mail something that large?" The sorcerer demanded. "Do you know how much that would cost? More than you're worth."

"You could shrink it!" Clodagh said hopefully.

"So, I will be using magic, won't I?" The sorcerer glared. "Don't just stand there collecting dust. Go fetch my cauldron and my ingredients. We have magic to do."

"Yes Master."

With a cauldron on a low fire, the sorcerer selected various ingredients from vials, jars and pouches, throwing them into the growing brew as Clodagh stood to one side stirring the mixture with a long handles copper spoon. He muttered and argued with himself as he worked, first selecting one mysterious powder, and then changing his mind. Once or twice he consulted a scroll or a spellbook.

"We must be careful, Clodagh," the sorcerer mused. "Something we have done has alerted the Ministry of Magical Artifacts. Were you careful when you brought my pets from the station?"

"No one followed me, Master," Clodagh replied. "I followed your instructions to the letter, waiting until high noon before loading the wagon, and I only took the back alleys on my way home."

"Hmmm," the sorcerer nodded, stopping to rub a finger along his nose as he gave the matter some thought. "It must have been the Abalaxia 47. I never should have used Orcs to acquire it, but good help is hard to find these days. No matter. Soon their agents will disappear with the bureau none the wiser for having sent them."

"Yes, Master."

"It would be far better if I could kill the two and leave the Witch's welp alive and discredited," the sorcerer continued, "but that would be too risky. Better, my dear Clodagh, to delay your revenge rather than risk your entire plans."

"If you say so, Master."

"Oh, Clodagh, I do say so. No matter how that

nosy witch has harmed me in the past, Esmeralda will get her just rewards in the end, whether they come now or later. We will soon have the power, my dear assistant, to bring the entire government to its knees. And then those fools will see what a mistake they made when they crossed paths with me."

"Yes, Master." Clodagh paused, looking down at the potion in the cauldron. "Do we not already have enough monsters? Would it matter if we do not have these last few shipments?"

"When going up against the Council of Magic, one can never have enough monsters," the sorcerer replied. "No, we will need these last few shipments and several more before we will be ready to make our move. But have no fear, when we do the whole world will tremble before my might."

Chapter 10

It had been a miserable few days. They were getting nowhere with their mission, and every morning Portia had to wrestle with the Mixmaster to prepare potions for Rhys and Lacy. So she was pleasantly surprised when a package arrived from her mother.

"Oooh," Lacy squealed. "A care package from back home. Hurry up and open it."

"It's my package," Portia laughed. "And knowing my mother, it's probably another textbook."

"I know but I so love surprises. I don't even care if it's not for me."

Still laughing, Portia unwrapped the gift from her mother. Inside, she found a funny-looking plant with a small flower like that of a Venus flytrap surrounded by vines so tangled they reminded her of a tangle of thorn bushes.

"That's strange," Portia commented, "it's not like my mother to send something like this. Oh well, it certainly is ugly."

"Well, I think it's cute," Lacy said. "And we can keep it right here on the counter so the Mixmaster doesn't get lonely."

"Does it eat spell components by any chance?" The Mixmaster grumbled.

"Just finish micing this last bit," Portia said. "If these two don't drink their potions soon we'll never get to class on time."

"Auug," Rhys groaned. "Those potions make me feel funny, and they task like my Aunt Petunia's old socks."

"It serves you right for forgetting your booster potions," Portia glared. "You know without it you would be biting every young girl in sight."

"Yeah," Lacy sniggered. "And at least you don't end up with an extra tail every time you sneeze. And you all know I'm allergic to humans."

"I've adjusted the formula," Portia said. "I think I've eliminated the side effects this time."

"Let's hope so," Lacy giggled, raising her mug to Rhys. "Bottoms up old bean."

With a hiccup and a belch, the two set their mugs on the counter and waited. When nothing happened after a count of ten, they counted themselves lucky. These potions were really beyond a 3rd class witch, and Portia was barely that. If she didn't permanently turn them into toads, then it was a good day.

Morning classes passed with relatively few

incidents. Once Lacy hiccupped and sent pink and purple bubbles drifting toward the ceiling of her classroom. As side effects go, she decided, it was rather pretty. When they all met in the atrium no one else had anything to report.

"We're getting nowhere on our mission," Rhys complained.

"I keep telling you," Sayd said. "it's all got to do with those trophies."

"You keep telling us that," Rhys complained, "but when we ask you how all you say is I don't remember."

"Yeah, go tell it to your mother," Portia snorted. "We're part of those thousands who don't believe you. Wandering about the school, causing mayhem wherever you go, and then carrying back tales you can't remember the next day. If you did see two shadowy figures confessing everything, where was it."

"I don't remember."

"We all saw that same play on our crystal balls," Portia said, waving him off.

Nowadays, almost every home had a crystal ball for remote viewing. The dramas were a big hit with the kids, while the adults tended to be drawn to the lectures and news shows. Only the week before they left for their mission the latest in the VanderClaven series had come out featuring that very plot.

"Forget about it," Rhys said. "Let's see what we can dig up in the cafeteria."

Shrugging, Sayd followed the others across the atrium. Directly inside the cafeteria doors, the four paused to look over the crowded tables. Rhys had spotted something. Sayd could tell by the glint in his eyes and the way he held his shoulders. If the vampire was hunting, Sayd was going to stick to his side no matter what. Unfortunately, what Rhys had spotted was not a suspect in the illicit sale of Ablaxia 47, but an apple.

The vampire pounced. Like a striking cheetah, he leapt on the overripe apple, Sayd following close behind. As Rhys sank his fangs into its flesh, a sloppy squirt of juice rocketed into Sayd's eye.

"By the exorcist's black heart," a thunderous voice cried. "I've been blinded!"

The cafeteria became pitch black, the windows rattled and the sprinklers came on. As Sayd went full poltergeist, Portia stumbled back, sitting heavily on the table and the sandwich that lay there. A squirt of mustard plopped out of the squashed sandwich and landed on the new hoodie of the girl sitting directly across the table. Blindly the girl picked up a dish of noodles and sauce and threw it. Landing one table over, the victims sitting there grabbed whatever came to hand and sent a volley in return.

For the second time in a week, a full-fledged food fight broke out in the cafeteria with an angry poltergeist in the centre. The whirlpool of his rage swept up items from nearby tables, spinning them out at reckless speed. Everything and anyone became a target. Pop splattered the walls, windows and floor. Pizza and burgers bounced off bodies. Tables and chairs were overturned, some of them still occupied. And through it all, Lacy, Portia and

Rhys tried to corral their irate friend.

"Sayd!" Portia shouted. "Smarten up!"

"Yeah!" Lacy said, "look at the mess you're making. Who is going to clean it up?"

"I certainly won't," Rhys declared. "I had nothing to do with it."

"That's not true," Lacy cried. "You were the one who squirted him in the eye."

"And I wouldn't have if her potions didn't have so many crazy side effects."

"None of this is helping," Portia seethed. "Will one of you please catch that crazy ghost!"

"Why do I have to do all the hard work," Rhys complained.

"Because you were the one who tried to turn an apple," Portia said. "Now catch that ghost."

Rhys had barely moved towards Saayd when the principal walked in. Suddenly the wind died down, food fell with a plop, and the sprinklers stopped gushing water. In the light, the wreckage was plainly visible. The principal had seen hurricanes and tornados leave behind less damage.

"Who's responsible for this catastrophe?"

One hundred fingers pointed at Portia, Sayd, Rhys and Lacy and a handful of others in the centre of the mess.

"All of you, to the office and wait for me there."

Reluctantly, they trudged through the wreckage and out into the atrium. Slowing their steps still further, they made the all too short walk into the office.

In the office, the receptionist pointed. "Go sit in those chairs and wait until the principal is ready for you. That was not very good adulating on any of your parts."

As they sat in the chairs, Lacy hissed, "this really is all your fault, Rhys."

"No, it wasn't."

"You're the one who squashed the apple," one of the other kids accused.

"I tripped and fell in the dark," Rhys lied.

"Yeah," a second kid remarked. "It's weird how it got so dark all of a sudden."

"Must have been a power outage or something," the first kid said. "Still, you're the one who started it."

"I told you I tripped," Rhys said, turning to glare at Sayd. "Someone else didn't have to have a hissy fit."

"I couldn't help it," Sayd sniffed. "That stuff burned my eye. It still hurts."

"You know," the second kid said, "none of this stuff ever happened when we had a security guard."

"Yeah," the first kid agreed. "Whatever happened to Al anyways?"

The four shared a guilty look, knowing he and the others lay trapped in the crystal orb in their lair. Panicked, they wracked their brains for a believable excuse. Rhys was the one who spoke first.

"Oh, he retired. I mean he was ancient. He had to be at least two hundred."

"No way dude," one of the kids laughed. "If he were two hundred, he'd be dead for a hundred years.

"Then he must be a hundred," Rhys said. "Either way, he retired and moved to Ghana."

"Ghana! What's in Ghana?"

"He moved there to pursue his opera career," Rhys continued. "What? You never heard him sing?"

"No!"

"Oh, he could have been a big star if he hadn't given it up to take this job. I guess he just got tired of chasing all us kids."

"Natch," Lacy replied.

Chapter 11

"Hey, look at that guy!" Lacy said.

"Yeah," Rhys shrugged. "What about him?"

"Look at his foot," Lacy pointed. "I think he's turning into a monster."

"She's right," Portia decided. "That's definitely not normal. His foot looks like it belongs to a troll."

"Yep. Definitely troll-like," Sayd said. "I think we ought to follow him."

"Whoa! Slow down," Rhys held out an arm to slow the other boy. "Don't make it so obvious."

As unobtrusively as possible given the thinning crowds, the four followed their target across the atrium. When he went into the elevator, they turned as one, racing up the main staircase to arrive in position before the elevator.

"No running in the halls!" Some anonymous teacher cried.

It seemed these human teachers were everywhere, and never where you wanted them.

Frustrated, the four slowed to a half-run, hurrying as they watched the doors to the elevator open in the distance. Too far to catch up before their prey exited, they leaned up against the wall and waited to see what direction he would take. One of those annoying teachers stopped the boy not far from the elevator and began a long conversation. Unable to determine where he was heading, the four could only lean against the wall and waited. There even weren't any lockers nearby to give them an excuse to be there.

"What do you think they're talking about?" Lacy wondered.

"I don't know," Sayd said. "Maybe she's suggesting he lay back on the Ablaxia until his foot turns back to normal."

"I don't know who he thinks he's fooling with that giant white boot?" Portia sniffed. "He can't even walk properly without those two sticks."

"Maybe he does," Rhys responded. "Humans aren't exactly the brightest bulbs in the package."

The four waited until the teacher was done and watched as their target moved down the closest hallway. Hustling to catch up, they arrived in time to watch the boy take the first right, heading towards the upstairs washrooms.

"If he goes into the washroom we've lost him," Portia groaned.

"Why?" Rhys laughed. "Sayd and I can follow him inside while you wait outside."

Ahead, their target stomped into the boys' washroom. Sayd and Rhys waited a few minutes and followed him inside. They saw him in one of the stalls but could not see what he was doing. Was he taking more steroids? And if he did, would he turn into a monster right away now that the transformation had already begun? The two could only wait and see but at least help was close by. And if not, they could always take up the chase again.

From the washroom, the boy with the funny leg headed back down the hallway towards the ESL and art classes. Sayd and Rhys came out a few minutes later and followed the girls around the corner, where they had taken up position to watch their suspect.

"So, what happened in there?" Portia demanded.

"We couldn't see," Rhys shrugged. "He went into a stall."

"Was there anyone else in there with him?" Lacy asked.

"Not that we could see."

"Maybe he just had to use the facilities," Sayd suggested.

"Never mind that now," Rhys said, "he's getting away."

They followed the boy with the monstrous foot around a corner and down the stairs towards the tech hallway. As the boy limped through the doorway at the bottom of the stairs, the lights went out.

"Ouch!" Lacy cried. "Who stepped on my paw?"

"It wasn't me," Rhys said. "I can't even see where your paws are."

"Never mind that," Portia snapped. "Did

anyone see where the monster went?"

"I can't see anything," Sayd said. "It's pitch black in here."

"Maybe I can relight one of these torches," Lacy reached up with her lighter but she was too short.

"I don't think that's a torch," Sayd said, craning his neck to study one of the lights. "I think it's more like an oil lamp. You need to look for a wick."

"Rhys," Lacy said. "Give me a boost and let me take a look. I have one of the Humans' plastic fire sticks."

Rhys bent over and made a stirrup of his hands. Bracing herself with one hand on his shoulders, Lacy stepped into the stirrup and let him lift her up. A plastic sheet covered the light, and it took several minutes for the werewolf to figure out how it came off. Handing it down to Sayd, she fished the lighter from her mouth and ignite the flame. As the flame launched the glass of the fluorescent tube, it exploded and set off the sprinklers.

"Ugh!" Lacy shook water from her hair, "how come it always rains inside here?"

"Well," Sayd said, "our instructors did tell us that the Human world enjoyed some unpredictable weather."

"Hey you kids!" The head custodian barked. "What are you doing?"

"Uhm," Portia said, "trying to get the lights back on."

"If you see the lights out, you come get a custodian," the man said. "You don't monkey around with the wiring. Look at the mess you made. I've had enough of you kids and your messing around. Come get some buckets and mops and you can clean it up yourself."

He started to lead the way up the hallway with the four when he paused and turned. "I see you two hiding there. Out you come. You can help clean up too!"

Two students were standing behind the corner immediately inside the door. Sheepishly, they crept out of hiding, unaware of what was happening. Their protestations of innocence fell on dear ears, and soon they were wheeling a bucket and mop, following the four new kids into the flooded hall.

"This is bogus," the boy said.

"Yeah," Rhys agreed. "All we were trying to do is find out why the lights keep going out."

"It is weird," the girl said. "It never used to happen before, except for that time someone knocked over a hydro pole."

"This is going to take us forever," Portia moaned. "There must be a million gallons of water here."

"Two million," Sayd said.

Pushing a mop into the puddle, Lacy moved it back and forth and put it into the wringer as the custodian had shown her. A trickle of water dribbled into the bucked. Lacy frowned. "This will take us forever, that's for sure. What we need is a big wind to blow it out the door and dry the place out."

"If Ben was here," the boy said, "maybe he could get his father to lend us a shop vac. That's what we really need."

"Whatever happened to Ben anyway?" The girl threw her mop into the bucket and combed her damp bangs out of her face.

"Ben?" Rhys leaned against his mop. "I don't think I know him."

"You know," the girl flounced. "About this high with long hair."

The four exchanged guilty looks. There was a boy with long hair amongst those they had trapped within the orb. They searched their minds for a good story and came up blank.

"I don't think he's been here since the accident," Sayd said.

"What accident?"

"He fell and hit his head," Rhys supplied.

"And he had amnesia," Lacy threw in.

"And now he thinks he's Cousin It from the Addams family," Portia said.

"And he's run off to pursue a career as a concert kazoo player," Sayd finished.

"Wow!" The boy shook his head. "Something like that happened to the security guard. Well, it's too bad because I really think he could have lent us a shop vac."

It really was a good thing that Humans were so gullible, Portia thought. Back home no one would believe a human boy was as good-looking as Cousin It, no matter how much hair he had.

Chapter 12

Back in the lair, everything was not well. The spell on the man-eating plant had begun to wear off. It started in the tangle of shoots, one of them thickening to the size of a tree and lengthening in a spurt that knocked the Mixmaster across the counter. A second and a third soon followed the third slamming into the ceiling with a shower of splinters. Soon a forest of massive tentacles was joined by an oversized head, saliva dripping from its massive fangs.

"Man the battlements!" The Mixmaster cried. "We're being overrun."

"This is not a precipitous time for an invasion," the digital clock complained, spitting springs at an encroaching tentacle. "I just had my springs oiled."

"Have no fear," the phonograph sang. "I shall sing us a rousing march to keep up our morale."

A couple of 78s came flying across the kitchen, cutting off a shoot that threatened to outflank the Mixmaster. Battling valiantly to the side of a misplaced Easy Bake oven, it came back to back with the other appliance in the far corner of the kitchen.

"Do something grandfather!" The Mixmaster urged.

"I am far too old t be drafted into your war," the grandfather clock intoned.

"But not too old to be eaten by a monster plant," the Mixmaster warned.

"In that case, like all good refugees, I shall retire from the field of battle and hide in the closet."

"Oh, wait until our masters get here," the Mixmaster said. "They'll soon put paid to you, you villain."

Portia and the others followed a boy out of the school. This one had to be turning into a monster – he had green hair. He led them out to the street to a space the kids referred to as the smoking pit. The kid spat then stuck a stick in his mouth and lit it on fire. Only monsters breathed fire, as everyone knows, so this time they were definitely on the right track.

"Did you see that?" Portia hissed.

"Yeah," Rhys nodded. "He's breathing fire. Not so is that kid, that kid, and even that kid."

The student in question took a hit on his vape. When he exhaled, he enveloped everyone around him in a cloud of smoke.

A crowd of fire breathers, Lacy thought. "Be careful. Maybe they spit fire like a dragon."

"I'd hate to find out the hard way," Sayd said.

They settled in under the tree and began to study the nearby students, looking for signs of a link between the Otherworld steroids and their odd behaviour. The boy with the green hair noticed Rhys looking at him and glared back. Rhys quickly looked away, bending down to flick an imagined speck of dirt from his shoe.

"All they're doing is breathing smoke," Lacy complained.

"Heads up," Portia hissed, "here comes some more. Maybe we'll get some action now."

As the two groups come together, the boy with the green hair held out his hand. From the corner of his eye, Rhys caught sight of a was of colourful Human money.

"I think a deal just went down," Rhys whispered to Portia.

"What are you fairies whispering about?" The green-haired boy demanded.

Lacy barked with laughter. "We can't be fairies, silly. Everyone knows fairies have wings."

"Are you calling me stupid?"

"No," Lacy paused, confused. "Should I be?"

The boy in question was considered by most as the toughest boy in school He had a short temper and a large fist. He was the wrong person and this was the wrong time for Lacy to have a misunderstanding.

"You witch!"

"I'm not a which," Lacy grinned. "Portia is."

Sayd pulled Lacy out of the path of the fist that was aimed at her head. Denied a target, the weight of the blow pulled the owner of the fist into the tree.

"Oh," the green-haired boy threatened. "You four are so dead."

"Let's get out of here," Portia urged, not wanting to tangle with an enraged dragon, even in human form.

The boy leapt to his feet, chasing after the four but unable to gain ground while his pants kept slipping down to his knees. With Portia in the lead, the four raced like the wind up the sidewalk. While Portia always enjoyed running, fear made her legs feel leaden. And yet somehow she was still well out in the lead when they reached the main doors.

"Quickly," she breathed. "Let's duck into the library. We'll lose them by ducking into our lair."

"Good idea," Rhys panted. He was winded and did not know how much further he could run.

No teacher saw them as they sprinted across the atrium. Like always, there was never one around when you wanted one. Inside the library they paused, looking back to see if they were still being chased.

"Look!" Lacy said, "the green-haired boy is by the door. Oh, and someone is pointing this way."

The three dashed from the door, earning a glare and a dirty look from the librarian. Slowing down to a more sedate pace, they continued around the corner before slipping behind the bulletin board. Opening the door, they leapt out of the frying pan and into the fire.

"Masters!" The Mixmaster cried. "At last you have arrived to help us slay this great beast."

At the moment none of them felt like they could offer much help. A tentacle had wound itself around Portia's ankles and now held her upside down, Rhys had been batted across the room, and Sayd was currently doing battle with three shoots.

Their erstwhile allies weren't faring any better. Forced to abandon the kitchen, they were making a stand in the centre of the den. A volley of springs, half-baked cakes, records and a mysterious green liquid beat down a tangle of shoots. Two more tangles were closing in on either side and soon these four would be forced to retreat into the entrance hall. From there it was a short, sharp battle away from ignoble defeat and the abandonment of their home.

Portia zapped the vine holding her, falling heavily to the floor. Rhys and Sayd soon moved to join her.

"Don't hurt it, you guys," Lacy complained. "Come off it, you're scaring it."

"We're scaring it," Rhys retorted. "Have you seen the size of this monstrosity?"

"Oh, it's only a baby," Lacy scolded, threading her way through a tangle of shoots. "Did these big baddies scare you?"

"Watch out Lacy," Portia warned, "it hasn't eaten in weeks."

"Oh, don't be silly," Lacy giggled. "It survives on love."

"Would you please get out of the way, so I can zap it?" Portia seethed, exasperated.

"If she makes a pet out of that," Rhys said, "I'm moving into a broom closet."

"I think I'll join you," Sayd replied.

"Get your own broom closet."

"You two are not helping," Portia scolded. "Lacy, look at its flower. It's a meat-eater and we are the meat."

"Don't be a silly goose," Lacy laughed. "Plants don't eat meat, they eat water and sunshine. He's probably just trying to catch a few rays."

"And Bobs and Petes," Rhys threw in.

"Don't worry Mistress Lacy," the Mixmaster cried from where it was tangled in Portia's feet. "We'll save you."

"Ah, that's sweet," Lacy said. "But don't worry about me. See, that tickles."

At that moment a shoot was probing her left nostril. Probably looking for a brain, Portia thought, disgusted. Good luck with that. Some of the finest minds in the Otherworld have been looking for decades without success.

"For the last time, Lacy," Portia said. "Can you move away from that thing before it bites your head off?"

"Don't be silly," Lacy sighed her frustration. "Plants don't bite, they just give kisses like this."

A giant pink tongue was currently slurping away at Lacy's face as if she were a giant ice cream cone.

"How many licks before it bites?" Sayd asked. "I bet four dozen."

"No go, old chap," Rhys said. "I lost count at thirty."

"I hope you realize this means she's keeping it,"

Portia sighed. "And I have first dibs on that broom closet."

Chapter 13

It was a long night. Every time Portia rolled over it was to find that giant weed trying to squeeze into the room she shared with Lacy. And as soon as she fell asleep a stray shoot was either tickling her or shoving her off the bed. She knew it was a mistake to let the werewolf keep that monstrosity but without Lacy's help, there was no way to get rid of it. Portia still wondered why her mother had ever sent such a thing and was beginning to suspect that she hadn't. At the first opportunity, she would get in touch with her mother through her crystal ball and ask her about it.

In the morning Portia woke groggy and cranky and in dire need of a drink with plenty of acid. "Hey, Mixmaster, what's on tap today?"

"How does vegetable soup sound?" The Mixmaster replied. "If that doesn't strike your fancy we have vegetable slurry, deep-fried vine, julienned vine, mashed vine, and of course the ever popular plant juice."

"Don't be mean," Lacy frowned.

"Have you seen what it has done to my kitchen?" The Mixmaster prodded. "And you have the audacity to call me mean."

"He's only teething," Lacy defended.

"Ha!" Portia snorted. "I thought you said plants don't bite."

"They don't but that doesn't mean they don't have teeth."

Portia sniffed and grabbed her books. "Don't forget we have detention at lunch. And if you're keeping that weed, you need to clean this place up after school. We're not living in its trash any longer than we have to."

Two classes' worth of time was not a long enough period away from that crazy werewolf as far as Portia was concerned. She barely made it through her first class and a test on the periodic table. Humans knew nothing about the elements. Half were missing and the rest they seemed to make up as they went along. I mean, Portia thought, where was transmorphium, and how could you get by without any knowledge of ethrealia? Earth, fire, water and air were totally missing, and they were the four basic elements that even a grade-schooler knew. Like there was really an element called scandium, and who in their right mind would mess around with chlorine?

"Man you look angry enough to chew hornets," Rhys said by way of greeting.

"I am," Portia said. "We had a quiz on the elements in the Humans' potion class."

"That ought to have been easy for you," Rhys began to count on his fingers. "Fairy dust, toadstool spores, bat's wings…"

"Nope, nope and nope."

"Frog eyes?"

"Nope."

"Not even dog's breath?"

"Nope."

"Well," he said, "I'm definitely dropping it from my next year's schedule. These humans obviously know nothing."

"That's what I was thinking."

"But they know all kinds of things," Sayd said as he joined them. "Do you know they have these devices to talk to each other over distances without the need for magic?"

"Nonsense," Portia scoffed.

"I'll show you one," Sayd turned to one of the students. "Hey, do you have an apple I can borrow for a minute?"

"Sure," the student handed Sayd a piece of fruit. "You can keep it if you want to."

When he turned away Portia burst out laughing. "Ha-ha. Let's see you send a crystal with that."

"This isn't the device I was talking about," Sayd snorted. "I must have got the name wrong. I'm sure the girl who was showing it to me called it an apple."

"Maybe they do," Rhys teased. "The other day

I saw a human talking into a banana."

Still laughing, the trio settled in to wait on Lacy. They had detention in less than five minutes, and if she didn't come soon they would be late. Where could that girl be? Her class was the closest to the atrium, so she should have gotten here first.

Lacy came running up breathless and looking like she had been dragged around the block. "Sorry, I'm late. I took Fig for a walk."

"Matilda's stars, she's named it," Portia moaned.

"Looks more like it took you for a drag around the block," Rhys teased. Where did you take him anyway?"

"Oh, just out back," Lacy said. "And then one of those creatures with the bushy tails came by, and Fig decided to chase it. It really was annoying. Those things climb trees, and of course, Fig had to try it too."

"We better get going," Sayd said. "We don't want to be late for detention."

"I still don't understand why we got the same number of detentions as you," Lacy sighed. "You and Rhys started it, and you did all the damage."

"The vagaries of human adults," Sayd shrugged. "Who will ever understand them."

The four wove a path through the crowd of students towards the office, where they would sit on chairs for the next twenty minutes. Apparently, humans did not go in for flogging, and dunking chairs were a definite no-go. Humans, however, we big on sitting. You sat with your nose in the corner, or a room with an angry adult sitting at a desk. You sat in the office while waiting to get in trouble, and you sat in the office as punishment. Maybe what was supposed to happen in these chairs didn't work on supernatural beings.

"Ah," the receptionist looked up from her computer. "There you four are. Go have a seat with the others."

Around the corner were two or three tables where half a dozen students already sat. The four found chairs directly across from the others, and the two groups sat in stony silence.

"This is lame," one of the boys said. "I didn't even do anything. All of a sudden the lights went out and I got hit with a chair."

"Same here," Sayd said. "I only walked into the cafeteria when someone or something squirted me in the eye."

"It was hard to see anything in the dark like that," Rhys leaned back in his chair, preparing to pontificate. "Who started what and when, it might be one of those mysteries we never solve."

"Too bad Elliot wasn't there," another boy sighed. "That boy could see in the dark better than a bat. If he had been here, we'd know what happen soon enough."

"Whatever happened to Elliot anyway?" The first boy wondered.

The four supernatural agents shared a guilty look, doing some wondering of their own. Like, was it possible that Elliot was one of the students they had trapped in the crystal? Better to be safe than let questions like this fester. If you let the doubts fester, sooner or later someone would come looking for the missing students.

"I heard something about this Elliot," Rhys said. "What was it again?"

"Didn't he die of natural causes?" Portia supplied.

"Elliot's dead!" The second boy exclaimed. "I didn't even know he was sick."

"He wasn't. He was attacked by, uhm, bats," Lacy said, panicked.

"I didn't know bats could kill you," a girl cringed.

"Oh yeah. They kill six or seven humans every year. Elliot was attacked by a swarm of North American Moth bats. Suckes are about," as Lacy rose to show just how big, she knocked a trophy off the table behind her.

Everyone froze, looking down at the trophy as if it were the body of a recently slain murder victim. Several threw quick glances over their shoulders, looking to see if anyone had noticed.

"Did you break it?" The girl whispered.

"I don't think so," Lacy bent down to inspect it. "Was that dent always there?"

"Don't touch it!" The boy gasped. "Do you want to get expelled or worse?"

The Principal, having heard the clang from the far end of the hallway, came bursting into the office. Stepping around the corner by the reception desk, he stopped dead in his tracks. His beloved trophy lay on the floor where it had been dashed by some callous hooligan.

"Who did such an evil thing?" He thundered.

"It was an accident," Lacy stammered. "A mere

miswag of the tail as they say."

"An accident?" The Principal stormed. "You young people are always in a hurry, never watching what you are doing or where you are going."

"No harm, no foul, as they say," Lacy said. "Here, I'll pick it up for you."

"Don't touch that. Do you know how hard I worked to earn that?"

Lacy looked down at the label, reading. "Girls' Basketball Champions. I did not know you played. Congratulations on your championship."

"Thank you, I think. Now the lot of you, get out of here," the Principal cradled the fallen trophy. "Are you all right, my beauty? Did that mean girl scratch you? Let daddy find a nice, safe place for you."

Chapter 14

When the four finally got home that day a letter was waiting for Portia, having recently arrived by batmail. Anxious to see her marks, and nervous in the same breath, she tucked it into her robe. She knew it contained her marks, and more importantly, word of whether she made the top of her class or not. Her mother had graduated top of her class, and nothing less was expected of Portia if she was to follow in that great woman's footsteps.

"I think I'll go straighten my dresser," Portia called to Lacy. "Let me know when the kitchen's cleaned up and I'll come to help you with supper."

"Okie Dokie," Lacy replied.

By the lack of response from the others, Portia knew that they too must have received similar letters and were too preoccupied with their own worries to notice her unusual behaviour. In the bedroom she plunked down on her bed and took out the letter. For a long time, she sat staring at it in her hands, unwilling to risk disappointment by opening it. Once she read its contents she would know whether her life's path was set or whether she faced an uphill battle. As long as it remained unread, her future remained bright.

But she couldn't sit here forever. For one thing, your privacy in a lair was always limited, and nowhere was that truer than in a school lair. And for another, she was too anxious to wait any longer.

Portia merely glanced over her marks before turning her eyes to the all-important sentence.

"What?" Portia stormed out of her room, lightning leaping from her eyes. "Second! I got second in my class."

"Congratulations!" Lacy exclaimed, once again misunderstanding the situation. "Guess what? I got top in my class. Oh, we're in the same class. By Grendel, that means we're one and two in our class!"

"Your family didn't happen to donate money to the Academy, did they?" Sayd drawled. "Say for a new spell lab?"

"I don't think so," Lacy said. "Anyway, silly, we just got a new spell lab two years ago."

Rhys' eyes flashed. His family had donated that spell lab shortly before his third eldest brother had graduated. He had heard the rumours about his family buying their diplomas almost since his first day in the Academy.

"What makes you say something like that,

Sprout Boy?" Hee snapped. "Do you think maybe Lacy worked hard for the marks she got?"

"Come on, it's Lacy," Sayd snorted. "She needs help tying her shoes!"

"Knots are hard," Lacy admitted. "I don't normally wear shoes back home. I love the feel of cold stone on my bare feet, especially the floor of my advanced alchemy class. I could spend hours in there."

"Wait," Portia said. "You took advanced alchemy?"

"Yes," Lacy nodded. "Didn't you?"

"I couldn't fit it into my schedule," Portia admitted. "Besides, it was hard to get in. Pretty much every slot was reserved for some legacy student."

"Oh yeah," Rhys retorted. "They only got in because they're legacies."

"What academy do you attend?" Portia laughed. "Your oldest brother failed spellbind twice and still came in second overall. Wasn't that the year your family donated the new teachers' lounge? The one with the automatic bubbling cauldrons."

"That was merely a coincidence," Rhys sniffed. "My family has made donations to the Academy for decades for tax purposes. Our year-end and the end of the school year just happen to coincide."

"Oh, now," Sayd said. "That's a laugh. You have a sister who's so bad at curses that a blind turtle could evade them. Didn't she take op of her class right after your family put in the new belfry on the campus post office?"

"That year my family turned around the old

spellworks," Rhys sighed. "We donated to the Academy, the Preparatory school, and the opera house to make up for the rise in dividends. Better we spend the money where we see fit that give up too much to the council and see it wasted."

"Speaking of operas," Portia added slyly, "that reminds me of your fourth brother. Didn't he spend all four years at the Academy writing an opera for a group of sirens?"

"See," Rhys said. "That just proves my point. Rodric is brilliant. He took over the old broom factory, redesigned our top-selling model, and made it one of our most profitable lines of business. And he did that within two years of leaving school."

"Well, I think your family is very generous," Lacy said. "I love all the things they've given to the Academy."

"You would," Sayd said.

"Sayd," Lacy barked, "I think you are just being mean. In fact, you can make your own dinner tonight."

"News flash, dim-wit," Sayd retorted. "Poltergeists don't eat."

In the kitchen Lacy began sprinkling everything with salt, letting it spill all over the counter and the floor. Seeing this, Sayd disappeared into his room and re-emerged with a chemistry set he had found in the lost-and-found. He immediately began a set of experiments using silver nitrate. While some apotropaics were mere Human superstition, Sayd was allergic to salt and only feared Brussel sprouts, and only pure silver really bothered Lacy. But in a war of nerves and annoyance, both were powerful weapons.

Pretending not to be annoyed, Lacy threw a handful of salt in his direction. "Oh, sorry about that. I heard that salt is good for keeping bugs out and I thought I saw a rather big one in the living room."

"Some people are just childish," Portia said, taking a large clove of garlic from the refrigerator.

She moved into the living room and sat across from Rhys. Portia wasn't a great fan of garlic, merely tolerating it, but she knew Rhys hated the very smell of it. Seeing her peel the garlic, he began to fiddle with a box of popsicle sticks Sayd had picked up from somewhere. Soon he began shaping them into crosses, taking the arms together with small dabs of tar.

"There's nothing more relaxing than shaping things with wood," Rhys said through a fake yawn.

"Yeah," Portia took a juicy bite of garlic. "You should make some stakes, we might need some in the near future."

"Oh, I wouldn't worry about it," Lacy drawled. "If you keep eating that garlic your breath will kill everything within a mile of here."

"Using enough salt on those toadstools?" Portia snapped back. "Any more and they will be mummified."

"I like them this way," Lacy took a bite and almost choked. "It gives them a real tang."

"Well," Portia said airily, "they're all yours. I've kind of lost my appetite."

"It's all that snacking between meals," Rhys said. "You would think someone who came second overall in her class would be able to figure that out."

"It's because she only came in second," Lacy said, "and not first like me. A little slow, you know."

"And some people," Sayd commented, "are a little too full of themselves."

"Full of something anyway." Portia agreed.

Not long afterwards the group broke up, each finding a quiet place to brook and lick their wounds. Lacy stayed in the kitchen, where she commiserated with Fig and the Mixmaster.

"Mixmaster?" She asked. "Could you whip me up something to wash away all this salt?"

"Right away, mistress," Mixmaster said. "Hot or cold?"

"Surprise me," Lacy decided. "You know, I thought someone would be excited for me for making the top of my class. It's not easy. All those sessions with the private tutors, all those long hours in the labs, and the extra assignments."

"I'm excited for you, mistress," Mixmaster said.

"I bet my grandfather would be proud too," Lacy said, feeling homesick. "You know, I'm the first in my family to ever attend the Academy."

"And what a shining example you are to all of us," the Mixmaster declared. "Isn't that right?"

"Hum-ha-ha-hum," the plant responded.

"Truer words were never spoken," the Mixmaster finished her drink with a flourish. "And may I just add, she is the apple of her grandfather's eye. And the same must be said for her father and mother, and even her brothers and sisters."

"Thank you, Mixmaster," Lacy said. "You are the best friend a girl ever had."

Chapter 15

The sorcerer looked up as Clodagh knocked on the door of his study.

"Master, your guest is here."

"Then show him in," the sorcerer snapped. "Don't leave a man like that waiting at our door for all the neighbours to stare at.

Clodagh shrugged and turned to fetch the guest, thinking that their nearest neighbour would have to have the eyes of an eagle to see from five miles away. Had he shown him right in, the sorcerer would have scolded him for not announcing their guest. As it was, he got yelled at for doing just that.

It was a hard life being an Igor.

At the door, the Exorcist stood in a black cassock, his white collar visible only at the throat. He wore a wide-brimmed hat, tilted like a gunslinger's, and carried a black medical bag. The mere thought of what lay inside made Clodagh shudder. With a nod, he led the way inside and back up to his master's study. Clodagh did not like this business and the sooner he was free of this man the better.

"Please come in, sit down," the sorcerer rose to greet his guest.

"I got your message you left with the guild," the Exorcist grated. "You are in need of our services."

"So, what qualifications do you possess, sir?"

The sorcerer was on his fifth interview to find an individual to scope out the misfits messing with his operation. Finally, the sorcerer broke down and went on a hunt for an exorcist, someone who is considered an assassin in the Otherworld. This candidate, in particular, had piqued the sorcerer's interest. The exorcist stood tall and was so colourless that he was practically opaque. When he removed his hat, his hair, ivory in colour, was slicked back with a fine-tooth comb. He was garbed head to toe in black with a white clerical collar. The man seated himself in a bergère chair on the opposite side of the sorcerer's desk.

He intertwined his fingers on his lap. His head tilted as if he were puzzled. "You said you were seeking an exorcist willing to enter the human world, yes?"

"Yes, I need someone to seek out some insolent

beings who have crossed into the Human world," The sorcerer paused. "Not for me personally but a poor school in the human world. I'm afraid it is haunted by some escapees from our world. I thought it my civic duty to try and help out before we have an incident."

The Exorcist nodded, saying nothing. He had heard many such stories in the past, and they all came down to the same thing – someone had an enemy they would like quietly disposed of with little or no connection to themselves.

"I need a qualified individual capable of fitting in a human high school. I believe the individuals in question are hiding themselves at this school. "I doubt they will give you much trouble," the sorcerer pressed. "They are young and inexperienced."

"The price remains the same," the Exorcist croaked. "Forty pieces of silver."

Forty pieces of silver. The price was steep but really, how much would one pay to take over the world? The sorcerer drew a pouch from the folds of his robe and handed it to the Exorcist.

"I believe our business here is concluded," the Exorcist tipped his hat. "I will contact you when the deed is done."

His contracts often started this way, he thought as he made his way out the back door of the tower. Keeping to the shadows, he drifted towards the guild's portal. The Exorcist's contracts were often in the Human world, and the guild would provide him with both safe passage and a cover identity. For these services, they would take half his earnings, a sum still cheaper if he tried to do it on his own.   After all, black market portals were expensive to operate and often unreliable.

At the guild office, he deposited his fees. Better to leave the coins here, in the vaults that were more secured than those at the Ministry of Magic. Little things from home like a coin could blow your cover as quickly as a slip of the tongue.

Crossing over, even with a portal, was a ticklish proposition. One never knows where one would materialize in the human world, and on several occasions, the Exorcist had nearly been run down by a mechanical monstrosity. Today was no exception. He materialized in a pizza parlour during the lunch hour rush when half the population from the school across the street attempted to crowd around five tables. Fortunately, no one noticed him pop into existence, although his appearance did not go entirely unnoticed.

"Hey!"   A boy with green hair snapped. "Watch out, lamebrain."

Turning, the boy saw the collar and stammered. "Oh, sorry Father."

"And very well you should, my son," the Exorcist grate.

He needed to get out of this crowd. Many of the students turned to say hello, and two had stopped him to ask for his blessing. If this continued, he would still be here at Christmas – and then some student would probably insist he say Christmas Mass.

Outside, he paused to study his surroundings. The school lay kitty-corner from the plaza across a busy street. He set out, keeping a wary eye on the metal juggernauts along the way. Humans tended to hurtle along in these contraptions at breakneck speed, and the devil take whoever got in their way. The Exorcist had discovered that if he timed his arrival at the corner to correspond with another group waiting to cross, he had a better chance of making it to the far side in one piece.

Finally, the Exorcist stood before the front doors of John Paul II Secondary School, where his targets were reported to be. Entering and slipping into place was all about attitude. Look and sound like you belonged and that was how people saw you.

Inside, he paused to watch the ebb and flow of the students. Across the atrium a young girl hiccupped, the sound echoing in the vaulted ceiling. It was followed by a concussive explosion. Following her with his eyes, the Exorcist continued to watch the girl until she hiccupped again. A fireball leapt from her lips, concussing against a pillar a few feet ahead.

"If I am not mistaken," the Exorcist mused, "that girl is a werewolf. But what in the name of the seven levels of Hell is with the fire?"

He started across the atrium towards her when he was intercepted by the Principal. "Good afternoon, Father. Can I help you?"

"I have been assigned to this school," the Exorcist said.

"Ah," the Principal frowned. "I'm sorry. We usually only have a chaplain, and still do, so I wasn't expecting a priest."

"Our mutual friend sent me to deal with a problem the two of you have run up against," the

Exorcist replied. "After all, we wouldn't want anything to interfere with your winning ways, now would we."

The Principal swallowed hard. "I understand perfectly. Let me see if I can find an office for you to work in."

"Ah, yes," the Exorcist nodded. "Perhaps something that overlooks the cafeteria, where I can keep an eye on the students."

Portia had finished dealing out their power diminishing potions. Still not up to standard, but somewhat effective. Somewhat. Somewhat in the sense of Lacy hiccupping out fire and smoke. She hid herself in the back of the atrium but with every upheave came a flame, setting things ablaze. Rhys had to practically dance around her patting out every spark.

"Lacy, what the hell?" Rhys breathed through his sharp gritted teeth "You've got to be more careful."

"I am, you bloodsucker!" Lacy retaliated. "I can't control my hiccups and they hurt."

She pouted and slid down the glass block walls encasing the back of the atrium until she was head between knees. She placed a delicate hand on her chest and whimpered.

Rhys sighed in empathy. She was clearly in pain and not built to deal with this. "Okay, here," he leaned back cautiously and slipped a water bottle out from the side pocket of a nearby student's bag. "Drink this. It might help."

She reached up desperately, yanking it from his hands and began chugging until the bottle was a borderline drought. Lacy gave a sigh of relief between her knees, a puff of smoke exiting her breath. At this time, the exorcist had entered the school. One could hear the sound of his formal black shoes echo in the atrium. He had arrived in time to witness the smoke to Lacy's breath but not in time to see the fire. He shook his head in disgust assuming it was the smoke of a human world's addictive cigarette. Continuing his way to the office, he started scanning the area before running into the principal and shaking his hand.

Lacy and Rhys stared at each other anxiously. They certainly weren't expecting a priest to show up. Why was he here? Was this normal?

Meanwhile, Lacy was struck by a fit of hiccups. She spat fire in rapid succession until smoke came out of her mouth and nostrils in a giant plume.

"Hey!" A girl complained, "stop vaping in school."

"Sorry, didn't mean to," Lacy said. "I think I might have swallowed it. I swallowed something anyway."

"You know," the girl said, "you look a lot like a girl I know. Karlee."

"Well thank you," Lacy said. "I get my good looks from superior breeding."

"If you say so."

"I just did," Lacy frowned. "I think."

"She definitely looks like Karlee," another girl said. "I wonder why we haven't seen her around lately?"

Why did someone have to mention a missing kid while I am alone, Lacy panicked? Why were the others not here? And then she remembered that they were all fighting because she got top marks in her class, and that reminded her that she was the top student in her class, and more than capable of handling this.

"Hey, you actually do remind me of someone," a student said motioning toward Lacy, "Casey? No. Karlee! That's it! I actually haven't seen her around the past little while."

"You mean as in Karlee, the girl who ran away with the circus and became a professional acrobat until she was involved in a freak accident which led to her being shot into space by a cannon?" Rhys belted out. It was the first thing that came to mind but didn't seem all too convincing. "Some say if you look carefully, you can see her hanging off the handle of the little dipper."

The older student laughed. She definitely thought he was being sarcastic. Lacy and Rhys chuckled alongside her attempting to match her social responses. Lacy let out a painful hiccup and held her chest once again.

Soon, the laughter stopped, and the student once again became stern. "Please watch yourself in following school rules. There's no need to get yourself in trouble for something that can easily be done over there." She pointed out the windows of the school entrance.

A small circle of students could be seen in a huddle past the fence line with cigarettes in hand and puffs of smoke. Lacy and Rhys soon caught on. She didn't actually catch what was truly happening with Lacy. The two eyed each other in relief.

"Got it! Thank you so much." Replied Lacy.

There, Lacy thought. I handled that perfectly. And with that, she walked off towards the library and their lair.

Chapter 16

The boy walked by in the hallway, simultaneously attracting the attention of both Lacy and Rhys. Not only was he unusually large and well-muscled, but he had more hair than either had ever seen on a human. Almost werewolfish, Lacy thought to herself. The pair turned to look at each other.

"Let's follow him," Rhys suggested.

Lacy nodded. This was more important than any human language course, especially English.

This time they had found a monster for sure. Even the boy's arms were unusually long, almost dragging on the ground like those of a troll. His gait was uneven, causing his body to rock forwards with each step in a clumsy dance. He led them up the main staircase and up onto the second floor.

From here there were a dozen places he could go, and he continued straight ahead and took an immediate left, making the two trailing behind and wondering if he was not heading towards the upstairs bathroom. One thing they had learned since coming to the Human world is that humans did not necessarily head towards the nearest bathroom but developed a preference for certain facilities.

"If he heads into the bathroom we will have to separate," Lacy warned. "If he goes full monster, will you be able to handle him?"

"If he goes full monster," Rhys said, "I'm making a hasty retreat until the others arrive. No way I'm tackling that Frankenstein on my own."

Again Lacy nodded. All four of them could possibly take down something this size, however, she did not know if any of the others would show up after the fight they had had yesterday evening. Other than Rhys, no one else was speaking to her, and she herself was not talking to Sayd or Portia after all the mean things they had said. Perhaps it was time to contact the Ministry of Magic and have them send in a real team instead of a bunch of snotty school kids. Lacy wondered if adults behaved like this, reacting to every jealousy and imagined slight, backstabbing and creating drama at every opportunity?

The monster did not lead them to the bathrooms as the two agents expected. He stopped midway along the hall and entered the office near the chapel. What was going on here? Neither agent was familiar with this part of the school, tending to avoid the chapel because of its negative effects on supernatural beings like themselves. Could this be the source of the steroids that now plagued the school? The two leaned against some lockers immediately across the hall, having moved passed the office to a place where they could keep it under observation. The woman who had opened the door to admit the monster now closed and locked the door, the two of them moving out of sight within the office beyond – all of which seemed suspicious to Lacy and Rhys.

"What is going on here?" Lacy wondered.

"I'm not sure," Rhys said, "but I think we should watch this office and see if any more students who are transforming come to this office."

"I think you are right." Lacy nodded. "I think we might just be onto something."

The Frankenstein boy left the office and headed down the hall. Before the two could give chase the green-haired boy broke off from a group of friends they had seen at the smoking pit and knocked on the door to the same office. Moments later, the woman inside invited him in, and once again the door was closed and locked.

"What do you think of that?" Rhys asked.

"Definitely suspicious," Lacy said. "He's the one who was breathing fire yesterday, so we know he's taking Abalaxia."

"Let's give it a little while more," Rhys decided. "Next time someone goes into the office I will try and get closer."

"But not too close," Lacy warned. "There's a chapel right there."

"I'll be extra careful then," Rhys said.

Some minutes later the boy with the green hair exited the office and hurried up down the hall in search of his friends. Lacy and Rhys stayed put, keeping an eye on the scarce traffic in the halls, ready to pretend to be opening their locker if a teacher should happen by.

Next to come up to the office they were staking out was a girl from the basketball team. Whiskers poked out from her chin like the quills of a porcupine or an ogre, one eye kept wandering to the far side of her face, and her tongue hung out of the left side of her mouth. She would definitely transform, and soon. Once she entered the office Rhys moved towards the small table set outside the chapel. There was a book on it that they had seen others signed, and he pretended to be putting in a prayer request while keeping one eye on what was going on inside the office.

The girl had sat down briefly while the chaplain went to her desk and took something out of one of the drawers. Rhys glanced over to watch her as the chaplain straightened up and moved back towards the student, and then quickly looked away as her eye caught his. Continuing to pretend to write in the book, he looked up a second time to see the chaplain hand a small package to the student. Sure he had witnessed a deal for Abalaxia, he put down the pen, wiped a hand over the open page of the book, and backed away to rejoin Lacy as the basketball player rose to leave the office.

"Let's get back to the lair," Rhys hissed. "I think I've unravelled the whole case."

"Did you see something?" Lacy whispered back as they hurried away and down the nearest flight of stairs.

"Yes," Rhys nodded. "She definitely came to see the chaplain get some more steroids, and the timing fits. Isn't there a big basketball game tonight?"

"You're right," Lacy agreed. "What else could the chaplain be giving an athlete hours before the semi-final game?"

Before they could make their break a girl came up to them, asking, "are you two waiting for the chaplain?"

"No," Lacy said.

"Oh, I was hoping she would know where Tara has gotten to," the girl sighed. "You haven't seen her."

"Tara?"

"Straight blonde hair," the girl explained. "Often wears a kilt."

"Oh," Lacy glanced guiltily at Rhys, "there was a girl like that who went to school when my mother went here. Too bad about her, though."

"Oh, what happened?"

"She drowned in the pool," Rhys supplied.

"John Paul doesn't have a pool," the girl scoffed.

"Duh," Lacy laughed, "they obviously filled it in once a student drowned. You wouldn't expect anyone to swim in it afterwards, it might be haunted or something."

"I guess you're right," the girl frowned, wandering off in the opposite direction as the two made their escape.

The two made their way straight to the library, and from there back behind the bulletin board and into their lair. They found Portia and Sayd in the kitchen, leaning back against the counter as they watched the Mixmaster working away at some drink or other. Neither waited to say hello as they burst out with their news, talking over each other in a confused jumble until Portia raised a hand.

"I can't understand a word you are saying," Portia complained. "Who broke what case? And why does it matter?"

"No, silly," Lacy giggled. "We broke the case, our mission is almost over."

"It's the Chaplain," Rhys explained. "She has an office up on the second floor, and we saw four or five of the students who are in the middle of a transformation go into there, and each time she locked the door."

"There's nothing suspicious about locking the door to an office," Sayd said.

"We saw the green-haired boy, the one who's turning into an orc, go into her office," Rhys insisted, "and we're pretty sure she gave him a vial of Abalaxia."

"Yeah," Lacy said, "and when he came out he was looking decidedly more orcish. I think he even had patches of warty skin on his face, all red and blotchy like."

"We already know he's transforming," Portia snorted. "And there's nothing really suspicious about him interacting with staff and teachers here, he is after all a student at this school."

"Yeah, out in the halls and classrooms," Rhys said. "How many do you see meeting with a teacher or staff member behind a locked door? None. Plus, she gave something to every student who came into her office."

"So what," Sayd snorted. "That woman is the

chaplain, and chaplains are one of those Human do-gooders."

"Yeah," Lacy retorted, "Exorcists are priests, and they do all kinds of evil things."

Chapter 17

After fighting with Rhys and Lacy, immediately following lunch Portia and Sayd decided to skip class and do some investigation on their own. Listening to the nonsense those two brought back, they felt they could come up with a better suspect within minutes of searching. The pair decided that the best place to start was outside and to work their way inside. And the one place they had not looked was out in the student parking lot. So they headed out into the afternoon sunshine, leaving behind their human classes and the nonsense they taught there, nonsense that was obviously rubbing off on Rhys and Lacy.

The parking lot was one place they avoided because of the metal monsters that lurked there.

They were loud and smelly, and off took off in a squeal of rubber at breakneck speeds. And yet, many of those suspected of using Abalaxia 47 spent a lot of time here.

"This place makes me feel ill," Sayd complained. "It smells worse than Brussel sprouts."

"I know what you mean," Portia shivered. "There isn't an honest broom anywhere in sight."

"Well," Sayd said, "I don't see anything of interest here, why don't we head inside where it isn't so hot and bright?"

"It looks like he's feeding one of those beasts."

"I don't think so," Portia pressed. "It looks like he's taking something out of its back end. Are those vials and flasks?"

"You may be right," Sayd raised a hand and squinted in the bright sunshine.

"So you think someone has sold him the formula for Abalaxia 47 and he's now cooking up his own supply? You would use most of that equipment for brewing potions."

"Only one way to find out," Sayd decided. "We'll have to follow him and see what he's up to."

As they leaned up against a pole, watching, the Science Teacher continued to root through his trunk. He was sorting through things he had brought from home for a project he was working on with some of his advanced students and placing them in a box. Some of the heavier things he would leave here until he could get his students to help. And other things he decided they would not need after all, and those would remain in the trunk for another day or perhaps another project. To the two recovery agents watching, it looked like he was trying to hide his true intentions beneath a bunch of junk to through off anyone who saw him.

Finally, their quarry was on the move.

"He's coming our way," Sayd observed.

"Let him pass us," Portia said. "We'll make our move once he reaches the door."

Sayd nodded, turning to watch the door without leaving his position on the post. With his heavy box, their quarry made slow progress, the cumbersome burden creating issues while he attempted to open the door. Once he disappeared inside, Sayd came off the post and led the way towards the school.

"It looks like he's heading up the stairs," he said.

"That's where the potion labs are," Portia nodded her head thoughtfully. "If our hypothesis is correct, and he is brewing Abalaxia here at the school, that's where I would expect him to head."

Sayd stepped through the door and opened it from inside, holding it for Portia. After lunch, the side door leading to the parking lot was locked, and today was no exception. But when your partner was a poltergeist, a locked door was of little consequence. Waiting only until their quarry was at the top landing, the recovery agents made their own way up onto the second floor.

"He's turning right."

"Towards the potion laboratory," Portia said, raising a significant eyebrow.

They arrived on the second floor in time to see their quarry slip into one of the science rooms and lock the door behind him. Although these doors had windows, they were often blocked off with solid vinyl curtains to keep those in the hall from distracting the students inside. Frustrated by her own efforts to see around it, Portia did not object when Sayd poked his head through the door to take a peek.

She pulled him back through the door by the shirt, asking," what did you see?"

"He's setting beaks and stuff up at one of those potion tables," Sayd whispered. "He seems to be brewing something up, so you might just be right."

"We'll wait here until he comes out and see what he does next."

A half-hour later, the Science Teacher came out of his room, turning to lock his door. Portia and Sayd spun to face a locker, pretending to have trouble with the lock as they watched what direction he went. At first, as their quarry turned towards the stairwell, they thought he was heading back out to the parking lot. And then the Science Teacher took a right and headed down the hall.

"I wonder where he's going with that box?" Portia said.

"There's an easy way to find out," Sayd said. "Let's follow him."

"Lead the way."

Trailing well behind him, Sayd and Portia watched their prey stop at the head of the hallway and let himself in a door they had never noticed before. Still meandering along the hall, they peeked through the window of the door as they passed by. Coming to a stop a few feet down the next hallway, they stopped to stake out the doorway.

"That's strange," Portia said. "Did you see what I saw?"

"All those selves, and plants, and dirt," Sayd nodded.

"It makes you wonder if he's crafting his own spell components," Portia speculated. "And whether he was the one who sent Fig to destroy our lair."

"Oh, I didn't think about that. That would mean he knows all about the Other World, maybe even all about our mission."

As they stood, working themselves into a lather as they explored every disastrous permutation, a familiar boy with green hair came up to the door and knocked. A moment later their quarry opened the door and the two disappeared inside. Portia and Sayd slipped across the hallway and stepped closer to the greenhouse, taking up a position where they could hear what was going on inside. Strange noises emanated from the room, causing the pair to exchange startled looks. When he turned toward Portia, Sayd noticed a few approaching students and gave her the high sign.

"I wonder whatever happened to Jacob?" One of the students said. "I haven't seen him in ages."

"Oh, Jacob," Sayd replied. "He doesn't go to this school anymore."

"Oh," the student asked, "why, what happened?"

"You know how obsessed he was with global warming," Sayd lied. "Well, he finally finished that orange submarine he's been building for years and took off to emulate that ocean explorer, Jacque

Costeau."

"Last we heard," Portia threw in, "he was stuck under the Arctic ice with a walrus named Charlie. You know he's always wanted a walrus named Charlie."

Looking puzzled, the student raced off to catch up with her friends. As soon as she was out of sight, Sayd pulled Portia away from the locker and propelled her down the hall.

"A walrus in a submarine?" Sayd scoffed. "Do you know how big they are? They eat whales and elephants."

"Well," Portia sniffed, "I wasn't the one who got the colour of the submarine wrong. It's green, like in the Human song we learned in preparatory school."

The two rushed away towards their lair, anxious to tell the others all that they had discovered. Both were sure they had stumbled onto the break that would allow them to wrap up their mission any day now. And the sooner the better. This strange Human world was beginning to wear on their nerves, what with its brightness, indoor rain, and its lack of quality food. Everything was sugar and cheese without a tadpole slurry anywhere in sight.

The others were still in the lair when they returned. "Guess what?" Portia announced. "We've practically solved the case."

"I doubt it," Rhys scoffed, "but let's hear it anyway."

"No," Sayd said. "This is real, not lame like thinking the Chaplain is dealing Abalaxia. We actually saw one of the science teachers brewing up a batch of Abalaxia in the potions room."

"Abalaxia?" Lucy giggled. "And you tried it out yourself?"

"At least we think it's Abalaxia," Portia spoke rapidly in her excitement, "because when he was finished he met the green-haired boy in a strange room at the end of the hall – you know the one from the smoking pit who chased us the other day – and these weird noises came out of the room, like the kind you would hear coming from a laboratory of a mad scientist."

"The room or the boy?" Lacy asked, confused.

"What?" Portia stammered.

"Which one are you saying chased us?" Lacy demanded, "because I can't understand you when you ramble like that!"

"The boy from the smoking pit," Sayd explained, "the one who was breathing fire, he went into the strange room with the Science Teacher immediately after he finished brewing that potion."

"Now you're saying the boy from the smoking pit was brewing potions?" Rhys asked, being intentionally obtuse.

"No!" Portia snapped. "He was the one the Science Teacher gave the potion to, and we know he's turning into an orc."

"Funny," Rhys commented to Lacy, "isn't that the same boy we saw going into the Chaplain's office? And what did they say to us again?"

"Oh, yes," Lacy said, "it was all just a coincidence. And that with the number of students currently using Abalaxia 47 that such coincidences are bound to happen."

"Ah yes," Rhys concluded. "I believe they've stumbled upon another such coincidence. After all, students who attend this school are bound to interact with a teacher or two."

Chapter 18

"It was night. The lights were all out and the hallways were empty when a shadowy figure slipped through a side door. He had arrived a few minutes ago and had left his car parked at the far end of the lot, where the odd car belonging to a student attending a nearby college was sometimes left behind. For five minutes he sat in the car watching the darkness, nervous that someone would wander by and discover his presence. Assured that no one was around to pry, he made his approach and slipped unseen into the building.

Now that he was inside he wasn't so sure. It felt as if eyes were watching him. It had to be paranoia and a little nervousness. Who would be in the school at this time of night? After pausing briefly inside the door, he continued deeper into the school. He had taken the precaution of turning off the automatic lights before he left the school so that they did not light up his route to this clandestine meeting like a beacon.

He entered the area behind the stage through the music room, not too concerned about the cameras now that there was no one to watch them. Whatever did happen to that security guard? He had heard some silly rumour that he had run off to Finland to become a seal herder but then again the kids came up with all kinds of crazy stories these days. Drowning in a non-existent pool while teaching sharks to dance, eaten by moths, becoming a pro basket weaver, and even living with a koala bear in a pink submarine. He was much too busy these days to chase down every silly rumour circulating around the school, even if a number of students seemed to be strangely missing.

"It took you long enough to get here!" A voice from the shadows snapped.

"I had to wait until I was sure the custodians had left for the day," he defended. "We can't afford to have them wondering what I am doing her so late at night."

"And are we safe here?" The Exorcist asked, stepping out of the shadows.

"Access back stage is restricted," he returned, "and students are not allowed back here without teacher supervision."

"Ah," the Exorcist nodded. "And speaking of students, I've prepared a list of possible Ministry agents. I will need access to everything you have on their backgrounds – schools they went to, class schedules, clubs and sports teams."

"I'm not comfortable giving you access to such confidential information."

"Would you rather wait until they undo all our hard work?" The Exorcist pressed. "I'm sure the press would love pictures of us walking out in handcuffs."

He wouldn't like that at all. A criminal conviction would see him barred from the building and his beloved trophies. In a few more months this school would have won more trophies under his watch than any other school in the district."

"What if I suspend all the students on this list?"

"That wouldn't be wise," the Exorcist said. "For one, it would raise suspicion. Surely, one of the parents would complain to the board if you suddenly expelled twenty students, and the board would be bound to investigate. Secondly, we don't want to interfere with our client's merchandise."

"Merchandise?" He queried. "What do you mean?"

"You certainly must know what happens to those poor sods who take too much Abalaxia and are transformed?" The Exorcist gave the other mane a hard look.

"What? What happens?" He stammered. "I was told they would be returned in a few days as good as new."

"Ah," the Exorcist nodded knowingly. "So he told you that, did he? Well, it's too late now. You're in too deep and your only way out is to help me uncover the identities of the Recovery agents before they can do any more damage."

"Yes," he said, "I understand, but what is going to happen to the students?"

"It's better you don't know," the Exorcist said. "Just be content knowing they are better off where they are now."

"But if they don't come back there will be an investigation and by more than the Board," he began chewing on a nail. "The authorities are bound to come asking questions we can't afford to answer."

"I see," the Exorcist nodded. "That will indeed be a problem."

The two men fell silent, each lost in their own thoughts. Both wondered how they had come to this time and place and had either been honest with themselves the answer would have been greed – one for fame, one for money.

"We'll need to come up with an excuse," the Exorcist decided. "Some kind of event or trip that will keep them away until we can extract ourselves from the situation."

"First, I will have to stop giving the students this Abalaxia," he said. "Right after we win the basketball championship."

"If you think that is wise?" The Exorcist nodded. "About this other matter, any suggestions?"

"I think I can backdate some paperwork for a trip to tour some US colleges," he said. "Maybe some stuff about potential scholarship interviews."

"That will help for the short-term. And if any of

the parents call?"

"Well," he replied, "we'll have signed permission slips. If one or two of them are forged, I will promise an immediate investigation. I will then hold them off by saying we are having difficulty getting in touch with them. If the authorities get involved, they will be looking for the children down in the States and not here."

"Now we only have the agents to deal with," the Exorcist said. "I'm sure this Lacy is one of them, but Ministry agents are tricky."

"It's too bad you don't know her last name because I can't find a Lacy in our database. It may be a nickname the kids have given to her."

"No worries," the Exorcist assured him. "I know what she looks like. Sooner or later she will lead me to the others."

"How dangerous are these agents anyway?" He wondered. "Maybe I should have the school resource officer deal with them. We could do a student-by-student search to see if any of them have false identification papers."

"Not to worry," the Exorcist said. "That is why I am here – to deal with these Ministry agents. All we need now is a little bit of patience to identify them, and then I shall rid the school of them permanently."

He did not like the sound of that last word. There was no way he would condone murder, especially of a student. Almost he found the courage to say something, but there was something dark about the priest that made him hold his peace. He was sure if he did say the wrong thing he would find himself one of this man's victims.

Chapter 19

The only way to end this deadlock, Rhys decided, was to find the evidence that would prove he and Lacy were right.

"Hey girlfriend," he called. "How would you like to do a little sleuthing today?"

"Sounds interesting," Lacy giggled. "What do you have in mind?"

"How about going to investigate the Chaplain's office, see if we can't shake something loose?"

"Now I am intrigued," Lacy said.

"Well just wait until the other two head to class," Rhys leaned forwards to whisper, "and then we will slip out. We wouldn't want any dead weight with us."

Lacy nodded. To pass the time they broke out a game of Spiders and Bats, the one thing Portia hated and could not be played with an odd number of players. The object of the game was to get all your spiders into your home keep before the bats ate them. During one round the player controlled the spiders while the other controlled the bats. Whoever got the most spiders into their keep in the fewest moves won.

"Don't you two have class?" Portia asked.

"We have a spare," Rhys said.

"Yeah," Lacy said. "We have a substitute teacher so the other kids told us we don't have to go to class."

"Lucky you," Sayd said, collecting his books. "We'll see you at lunch."

The two did not finish their game. They waited for five minutes after the second bell and then slipped out of the lair. The Chaplain was only part-time so she did not come every day and today was one of the days her office lay empty. Rhys had checked her schedule out the day before to make sure the coast was clear. Now all he and Lacy had to worry about was being spotted by a teacher as they navigated the halls. Some of them appeared to memorize the schedules of every student as if they had nothing better to do.

"Be careful, we don't want to be spotted by anyone in the office," Rhys warned as they left the library. "We'll go left and take the far stairwell."

Lacy nodded and let him take the lead. Rhys stepped quickly through the atrium and did not slow down until they were well past the bathrooms. Now it was only a matter of climbing the stairwell and navigating the upper hallway. As long as the teachers along this hall were preoccupied, they should make it to the Chaplain's office safely.

"We need to keep a sharp eye out," Rhys said. "You watch the hallway while I pick the lock."

"Okie-Dokie," Lacy said.

Soon the two were in position near the Chaplain's office. Lacy leaned up against the far wall, where she could watch traffic from both directions. When the coast was clear, she gave Rhys the nod. The vampire set to work on the door using a set of lock picks he had inherited from one of his brothers. Over the decades they had been used by generations of his family to wander into the restricted areas of the Academy. Today he put them to good use opening the door of the Chaplain's office in the service of the Recovery Division of the Ministry of Magic.

"We're in," Rhys hissed.

Lacy quickly crossed to join him and quietly closed the door. Neither required light, both being creatures of the night capable of seeing in the dark. Rhys moved directly towards the desk, leaving Lacy to rifle through the shelves and a few boxes on the floor. Rhys ignored the computer, that being Sayd's thing and not his, and immediately opened the top drawer. Like that of most desks, it contained uninteresting miscellanea – sticky notes, pens, pencils, paperclips and a couple of items Rhys thought might be torture devices.

"Nothing here," he shut the drawer a little harder than he intended and winced.

"Here either."

"Keep looking, there's got to be something here."

Lacy thumbed through the books on the shelf, grabbing random ones and letting the fan open to see what might fall out. In the Otherworld, hiding important papers amongst the pages of a book was an old standard. Of course, it worked better when your library was a whole room full of thousands of books. She picked up a book entitled Diabetes and began thumbing through it. Lacy had no idea what it meant but the title, printed in a gothic font, caught her eye. Suddenly a page fell out of it and drifted to the floor.

"I found something," she whispered.

"What is it?"

"I don't know," Lacy held it one way and then another. "Some kind of list."

"Let me see it."

Rhys studied the paper for a long time, as puzzled as Lacy. There were times in one column and numbers and letters in a second. A note in the margin said something about blood sugar, which Rhys was sure was some kind of poison or even an anti-vampire serum.

"This must be a schedule of when to give their victims doses of Abalaxia," Rhys speculated.

"You think so?"

"I'm almost positive," Rhys pointed to the page. "You see this, this is times and those are the human's name for the days. They don't work off a lunar cycle like we do where each day has its own name. Instead, they repeat these every seven days."

"Sure," Rhys nodded. "But see this one? I think those cc's stand for a couple of cupfuls, and you take potions by the cup."

"Wow!" Lacy exclaimed. "No wonder that lot is transforming. I mean, two cupfuls what – one, three, five times a week. That's a lot for any kind of potion."

"Let's check the rest of the place," Rhys suggested, "and then head back to the lair."

Lacy returned to the shelves without much success, while Rhys went through the rest of the desk drawers. Several of them were locked and he had to resort to his trusty lock pick set. The effort was hardly worth it. He found nothing incriminating and had burnt his hand when he had accidentally picked up a Bible. Such books in and of themselves were not necessarily dangerous to his kind, but when they were actually read and used to pray by the faithful it imbued them with power. Like a static shock, when they were touched they delivered quite a jolt.

"let's get out of here," Rhys swore and stuck his burnt fingers in his mouth.

"You got to be careful," Lacy said. "A school like this must be full of traps. My teacher said this was a faith-based school, and then she even said a prayer. Can you believe it, a prayer!"

Checking the window of the door to make sure the coast was clear, they slipped out. Lacy was closing the door when a group of girls passed by.

"I wonder whatever happened to Nelly?" One of the girls asked.

The two looked at each other. Was one of those

trapped in the crystal named Nelly?   One the principle of better safe than sorry, Lacy spoke up.

"Oh, Nelly doesn't go here anymore."

"She doesn't," the girl backtracked to face Lacy and Rhys. "Why?"

"There was a skateboard accident," Rhys supplied.

"Nelly had an accident!"

"No, not Nelly." Lacy thought it was better if not all of them had accidents. That might seem suspicious. "Elizabeth Olsen. So they needed someone to play her role, and Nelly was lucky enough to get the part."

"Unfortunately for Elizabeth," Rhys embellished. "Nelly was so much better at the part they say they want to keep her."

"I'm surprised you haven't read about it," Lacy said. "It's all over social media. I mean, it's not every day someone from this school, let alone London, makes it so big."

The girls walked off excitedly pecking away at their phones.

"I think you overdid it with the last part," Rhys warned. "What if they look for it on their fruit devices?"

"I wouldn't worry about it," Lacy waved away his objection. "This internet thingy is so big no one can find anything on it. I heard one of the boys tell that to our teacher when we were doing a research project in the library."

Chapter 20

"As soon as those two are preoccupied with their game," Portia whispered to Sayd, "we'll pretend we are on our way to class, and then we'll slip away."

The pair were in the kitchen, leaning against the counter as they waited on the Mixmaster to make them a drink. In the living room, the others were starting a game that Portia thought too childish to be worth playing – Spiders and Bats. It would start slow and would take several minutes before it became complex enough to engross their attention. So they sipped on their teas and waited.

"Now," Portia hissed, calling into the living room. "We're off to class."

"Yeah," Rhys yawned, "Lacy and I are just going to finish up this game. See you at lunch."

"Not unless we see you first," Sayd called as he followed Portia out the door.

In the library they checked their surroundings, making sure no one had seen them leave their lair. Once reassured, they headed out and fought the flow of traffic down the hall towards the parking lot door. They had decided to hide out amongst the tall pines until the second bell sent the students to class, and then search the lot for the Science Teacher's car. There was no guarantee that he would park in the same spot, so they were prepared to search the lot if necessary.

Once outside and ensconced amongst the trees, Sayd sank back against the trunk with his hands behind his head.

"You look comfortable," Portia scolded, "but we are not out here for pleasure. This is work."

"Might as well enjoy it while we can," Sayd replied. "We go a good half hour wait before everyone will be engrossed in their classwork."

"I guess you are right," Portia sank down beside him. "Might as well enjoy it while we can. They don't get too many gloomy days in the Human world. I think it's been sunny and bright every day since we got here. I don't know how they can stand it."

"You know, I believe you're right. Seems it only rains inside here."

After enjoying the cloudy day with its lowering sky, the two were close to falling asleep when Portia decided it was time to get started. Together, they wandered into the parking lot and amongst the cars in search of one particular vehicle. The first place they looked was where they had seen it yesterday and found it missing. Fortunately, it wasn't far. The Science Teacher had found a parking spot near the centre of the lot, and chose to park there because he did not have anything to carry into the school this morning.

"Shivers," Portia cursed, "it's locked."

"No worries," Sayd slipped through the windshield. "Hang on while I figure out how to unlock these doors."

Sayd picked at the door, pushing and pulling at every button. Finally, he pulled something that popped the hood.

"Never mind," Portia said. "Let's check in here first. He took everything out of the back end of the beast anyway."

Portia really did not want to crawl into one of these metal beasts. She still wasn't sure what they ate, but she suspected they slowly drained the life force from anybody who climbed inside. She wasn't willing to risk it. Sometimes ignorance was bliss despite what her teachers said both here and in the Otherworld.

"Let's see what we can find in here," Sayd drifted through the back windshield to join Portia.

"These are definitely beakers," Portia said. "And that's a mortar and pestle, the kind we use to grind ingredients for potions. This is definitely an alchemist, witch or sorcerer's equipment."

"What's this?" Sayd picked up a plastic container and read the label. "Ni-tre-ates"

"It's one of those fake elements I think," Portia said. "I wonder if it's a substitute for one of the ingredients for Abalaxia. Or maybe a different name for one of the ingredients."

The pair continued to root through the trunk of the car, finding many items they had no idea what they were for or what they did. And then Sayd discovered a cubby hole with one of the round legs from one of the beasts.

"I think we discovered what these things eat," Sayd said. "Other metal beasts."

"The larger ones must feed on the smaller ones," Portia nodded in agreement. "It must be saving this piece for later."

"Well," Sayd said, "we will have to look inside."

"You do it," Portia said. "It'll be quicker if you searched than if you wasted all that time looking for a way to unlock the doors."

Portia still didn't want to climb inside one of these metal beasts, even if they thought they knew what they ate. There was always the off-chance they were only cannibals when their preferred prey was not available, like many wild species in the Otherworld.

Sayd, meanwhile, had climbed back into the car. He decided to start in the back seat since he had popped in through the rear windshield and was already there. On one of the seats, he found a bag.

"Hey, look at this," he called.

"What is it?"

"Looks like sage," Sayd winced and sneezed. "And a bunch of other herbs and such."

"Well, keep it away from me," Portia took a step

back from the car. "That other stuff, like the witch hazel, is used in potions. Sage, however, is one hundred percent an apotropaic."

"A pot of what?"

"Apotropaic," Portia explained. "A potion or artifact that kills or harms people from the Otherworld."

"Oh my wizard gizzards," Sayd squealed. "There's two bags of salt in here"

"Quick, get out of there while you still can!" Portia warned. "I think the Science Teacher is not only selling Abalaxia, he's on to us and is trying to get rid of us."

In his panicked state, Sayd had a tough time slipping through the car door. Stuck, Portia had to grab his arm and the back of the shirt, pulling for all she was worth. When Sayd came free with a loud pop, she fell back onto the seat of her pants.

As the two picked themselves up and dusted themselves off, Portia overheard a girl ask, "isn't it weird, Sarah hasn't been here for so long. Have any of you heard from her?"

"Oh Sara," Portia said. "Oh yeah, she had an accident during her ballet recital."

"Oh dear," another girl exclaimed. "Is she alright?"

"Well," Sayd said, "it depends on your definition of alright. She fell off the stage and into a spontaneous black hole."

"A black hole?"

"Oh yeah," Portia nodded. "They say she's still dancing on the event horizon for all eternity."

"I've never heard of anything like that before," a

girl said suspiciously.

"Sure you have," Sayd scoffed. "That famous singer wrote a song about her, what's his name, Elton John."

"What song?"

"Tiny Dancer," Portia said.

"Wait a second," one of the girls glared. "Isn't that singer a dinosaur, and that song older than the hills?"

"Of course, it is," Sayd laughed. "It's a time paradox. All black holes cause time paradoxes. Even though Sarah only fell into the black hole a week or so ago, they have been able to see her dancing on the event horizon for decades."

"I still don't think that's right.

"Oh, you know how the song goes," Sayd teased. "Tiny dancer, something, something, dancing forever."

"That sounds like Tina Turner."

"It would," Portia said. "I'm pretty sure it was a duet."

Somehow the girls were not convinced about the song, but happy to finally know what had happened to Sarah, the group of girls headed off for lunch.

"Well," Sayd said, "I think we handled that one pretty good. Should be no more questions about Sarah now."

"Yeah," Portia agreed. "We better hurry if we are going to meet the others for lunch. First bell has already rung."

Chapter 21

"Guess what?" Portia and Rhys cried at the same moment. "We have proof the culprit is the -."
"Science Teacher."
"Chaplain."
The two groups had arrived simultaneously moments ago, prepared to spend the lunch hour together in their lair. Now they faced off against each other a few steps into the living room.
"No, it's not!" Portia snapped. "It is the Science Teacher."
"You won't say that after you hear what we found out about the Chaplain," Rhys waved off her objection.

"And you won't say that once you've heard what we've found out about the Science Teacher."

Still glaring at each other, they moved to sit on opposite sides of the U-shaped sectional couch. Sayd and Lacy move to join them, both sitting in the corners at the base of the U.

"We got into the Chaplain's office," Rhys said.

"Yep," Lacy shook her head. "We broke in and searched it top to bottom instead of going to our morning classes."

"Well, we searched the Science Teacher's mechanical beast," Portia shot back.

"Whoa!" Lacy gasped. "You went into a mechanical beast?"

"Well," Sayd said. "I did. Portia stayed outside to keep watch."

"What was it like?"

"Scary," Sayd admitted. "At one point I did not think I would get out alive."

"Never mind all that," Rhys snapped. "We definitely found proof that the Chaplain is involved with the Abalaxia. In one of her books, we found -
."

"I found it," Lacy said proudly.

"Yes," Rhys continued, "Lacy found a list that I recognized as a dosage schedule."

"So," Portia snorted. "In the back of the mechanical beast we found plenty of tools for making potions, and inside we found sage and salt – ingredients for making apotropaics."

"I found that, actually," Sayd said. "Portia didn't go inside the beast."

"And I don't blame her," Lacy said reasonably.

"That's neither here nor there," Portia said. "What we found in his beast definitely points to his involvement in the Abalaxia problem."

"Abalaxia 47 is a potion, right?" Lacy asked.

"Of course, it is," Rhys sighed.

"Well," Lacy said, "I think Portia may be right."

"I don't know," Sayd drawled. "This dosage schedule seems like pretty solid evidence to me."

"See," Rhys smiled smugly, "even Sayd agrees with me. Between her handing things to the students who are beginning to turn, and the dosage schedule the evidence is mounting against the Chaplain."

"Well," Portia said, "Lacy agrees with me. Between his making potions and meeting with students in that little room, and the equipment and ingredients we found in his mechanical beast, the evidence is much stronger against the Science Teacher."

"How do you know those things don't belong to the mechanical beast?" Rhys demanded.

"He's got a point," Sayd said. "What do we really know about those mechanical beasts? Maybe they own humans and not the other way around."

"It seems very unlikely," Portia scoffed. "They don't even know enough to come in out of the sun – it's always fading their colour. And the other day I saw two of them charge headlong at each other. There were mechanical beast guts all over the place."

"That doesn't seem so smart to me," Lacy agreed.

"And another thing," Portia said. "How do you know it's a dosage schedule? You don't know the first thing about making or administrating potions."

"She has you there, Rhys," Lacy giggled.

"First of all, I do know all about the Human calendar system," Rhys retorted. "More than enough to recognize a weekly schedule. And what else could cc stand for if not a couple of cupfuls?"

"Ah," Sayd said, "definitely a good point, my man."

"What if it's a conspiracy?" Lacy asked. "You know, maybe they're both involved. One is cooking the potions and the other is distributing it."

"Don't be a daft bat," Portia said.

"Really, how human could you get," Rhys agreed. "It's obvious that I am right."

"There's no reason to be rude!" Lacy barked. "If you two were so smart, you'd have come in first in your class instead of me. How does it feel knowing you're not as smart as a daft bat?"

Lacy got up and stormed into the kitchen. She slammed cupboards and doors, and rattled cutlery, purposefully ignoring the others.

"It sounds like you could all do with a break," the Mixmaster perked up. "How about a nice refreshing drink, say a round on the house?"

"I'd rather choke on chocolate than share a drink with that lot," Lacy sulked.

"Doesn't a nice, hot swamp mud slider sound good?" The Mixmaster pressed. "Something to soothe all those ruffled scales."

"They're nothing but a bunch of wart toads that deserve to frown in swamp mud!" Lacy shouted.

"Who are you calling a wart toad, hairball?" Portia questioned sharply.

"If the name fits, wear it!"

"Girls," Sayd smirked at Rhys. "They get upset too easily."

"You're right," Rhys nodded. "You wouldn't even bat an eye if I called you a plague rat."

"Nor you," Sayd said. "If I were to call you a turnip sucker or a blood-deprived leach."

"You know," the Mixmaster piped up, "it might be a good thing if you all come and cool down, say with a nice cup of iced arsenic tea?"

"Cattle-tipper," Portia snapped.

"Broom-jockey!"

"Or the son of a drunken albatross."

"Or a jilted bat," Sayd laughed.

"Really, masters," the Mixmaster pleaded. "No good will come if you continue this."

"Gamey-legged sea hag!"

"Snail snot!"

"Blood-corrupted Wight!"

"Brussel sprout!"

And then it happened. The lights went out and a banshee's wail shouted the alarm. Tiny fairies strobed colourful lights that filled the lair as an invisible hand pushed them to the four corners of the room. A line lit up, pulsing as it glowed in the dark. A second joined it, dividing the lair into four parts where they intersected.

All four had her the legend. Any schoolchild living in a lair had, but until that moment none of them had thought it was more than an urban legend. Trapped in a quarter of the lair, unable to see or hear the others, they each railed at the injustice. Finally, exhausted, they retreated to a corner or other hidey-hole to lick their wounds and nurse their wounded pride.

The next morning the four were called down to the office and given detentions. Apparently, the humans had some sort of magical system to tell who had attended their classes and who hadn't Portia wondered if this too was stolen from the Otherworld, and wanted to ask the others what they thought. Unfortunately, the Time Out barrier was still not letting them talk to each other. So here they sat, staring at each other across a table in total silence.

"This is ridiculous," Portia sighed. "We're Recovery Agents working on assignment for the Ministry of Magical Recovery division and we can't even speak to each other"

"You're right," Lacy said. "I'm sorry I called you swamp slime."

"And I'm sorry I called you a daft bat," Portia laughed. "Wait, when did you call me swamp slime."

"Just now, I guess," Lacy laughed. "Frankly, I forgot what I really said."

"Me too."

And as they laughed together the girls realized they still could not hear the boys. Something about the apology had brought down the barrier, Portia and Lacy decided. Neither girl was ready to apologize to the boys, and apparently, they were not ready to apologize to them. Let the silence reign between them for a few more unholy hours.

Chapter 22

As the four came to the top of the stairs, they continue through the hallway. Sayd has thought it would be funny to push Lacy into the boy's washroom. After all, what harm could it do? Suddenly he gave her a shove, and Lacy went flying through the door. She fell to the floor in a heap. As she looked up, she came face to face with a -.

"AHHHHHHHHH!" Lacy wailed.

Sayd, Portia, and Rhys rushed into the washroom, ready to rescue Lacy and give battle to whatever was attacking. They skidded to a halt. They were faced with a blob of human flesh with a finger sticking out of it.

"Ew!" Portia frowned.

"What are we gonna do, people are gonna start to come towards the washroom?" Lacy wailed as she got up off the floor.

"I'll go find an antidote while you guys stay here. And please, make sure no one sees this mess!", Portia panted, running through the door.

"Okay", the three said in unison.

"I'm gonna stand outside and make sure no one walks in here," Rhys rushed out of the boy's washroom.

"Alright, we'll try to contain this blob but it's not going to be easy", Sayd gave an exaggerated sigh.

Portia sprinted through the hallway trying to get to the lair as fast as possible. She skidded down the stairs, nearly toppling head first as she raced towards the library.

"Hey, no running in the halls!" the principal yelled from across the hall.

"Yeah, whatever," Portia rolled her eyes. Humans were always getting in the way, and never where you needed to be.

Inside the lair, she rushed around trying to find her backpack.

"Ugh, where did I last put it?"

She rushed around from room to room, checking in closets and drawers, under the bed and the dresser, and even behind the grandfather clock. Where are you hiding, you dumb hunk of rotting leather? Portia always placed it on the chair by the door when she came back to the lair but it never stayed where it was put. Once she had found her bag hiding in the refrigerator, and another time in the shower behind the mud cakes. It was as if it knew she was looking for it, which it did, and was refusing to give her back her things as it did on almost a daily basis. This time for sure she was selling it to a dragon feed factory!

"There you are!" Portia exclaimed with an exasperated sigh.

As Portia moved to get it, the bag ran away.,

"What the? Come back here! Stop!" Portia yelled as she gave chase.

Its flight ended up behind Lacy's man-eating plant, reaching safety while Portia's back was turned, where she had seen it dash in beneath the couch. She poke around, wondering where her backpack could have possibly gone. She had only turned for half a second.

"There you are", Portia whispered with a sly chuckle.

Tiptoeing towards the backpack wasn't the smartest plan she had with the man-eating plant in front of it. Like a puppy, it liked nothing better than to play. And fetch and keep away were two of its favourite games. The plant leapt from the corner, its straight sharp teeth, almost like those of a Venus flytrap, chomping as it launched itself at her.

"AHHHHH! Back away!" She swatted at the monster.

Tendrils reached out to tickle her, chasing her back a foot or two. Portia dodged in, trying again to snatch up her bag as it stuck its tongue out at her.

" You know what?" Portia scoffed as she grabbed a fairy splatter near the front of the entrance. "I think I've had just about enough of this game. We'll be having beanstalks and fried leather for dinner."

Portia gave the plant a whack and backed it into

a corner. As her bag made a break for it, she swung again, sending it crashing against the wall with a loud splat.

"Phew! Thank you," she said, blowing the hair out of her face.

Stalking across the room, Portia snatched up her backpack with an extra hard tug. " It's almost like you already know what I needed.   Is that why you were running away, you spawn of an imp? Well, this is for thinking you can run away from me!"

Portia laughed. She wrapped her arms tightly around the bag and choked it hard. "C'mon, spit it out! You know what I need.   I'll turn you into an old pair of boots if you don't give me what I want".

With a very loud gurgling sound the backpack spat the antidote out, where it landed a couple of metres away from her.

"Finally! Thank you,"   Portia sighs as she dropped the backpack.

She really needed to replace that senile patch of leather, Portia thought as she picked up the antidote and pulled the cork out of the beaker and sniffs it. This will do, she thought as she ran out the door, racing to rejoin the rest of the group.

Meanwhile, things were not going well upstairs near the bathroom. The blob kept pushing Sayd and Lacy towards the door, while Rhys was faced with an angry crowd wanting to get in before second bell.

"Can you move out of the way already? I need to go to the washroom," a JPII sighed.

"I already told you, the custodian is cleaning,

there was a huge spill and it's gonna take a while for it to get cleaned up", Rhys said, rolling his eyes.

"Then why isn't it locked", the boy stomped away, leaving some choice words for Rhys to chew on.

Rhys opened the boy's washroom door "How is it going in there, guys?"

"As well as it can", Lacy said. "It' keeps growing, and that's the least of it. If it gets any bigger it will cave in one of the walls.

"To be honest it doesn't do much, it just sits there", Sayd shrugged, raising an eyebrow and tilting his head. "I've never seen a more uninteresting monster.

Rhys closed the door and took up position once again.

"Hey," a girl walked up to Rhys.

"Um hey."

"Have seen a girl named Ranah around, because she's supposed to be my lab partner but I haven't seen her?" The girl sighed in frustration. "We have an assignment due next class, and no one's seen her in over a week.

Rhys started to get nervous and tried to think of a lie to tell her. "Um. Actually, I heard that she had fallen somewhere."

"She fell somewhere? Well, where?" The girl laughed

"Well, she fell a couple of blocks away from this school actually. I think it was on her way home. She fell in the crack of the sidewalk," Rhys elaborated as he scratched his head.

"You really think I'm going to believe that?"

She laughed.

"You know if you go to the specific crack she fell in, you can still hear her scream," Rhys said with a very serious look.

The girl speed-walked away with the most terrified look on her face. Once she's completely out of sight, Rhys dragged out a long sigh and walked into the washroom. Once he's in, Lacy and Sayd looked at him with fright clearly on their faces. "What's wrong?"

"Ummmm, so basically the blob started leaking and now we don't know what to do because it is starting to get a little frisky if you know what I mean," Lacy rambled

"Okay, calm down. Nothing is gonna happen," Rhys said. "Let me see what I can do."

Meanwhile, the blob of flesh bounced in all directions, sending a spray of goop in every direction. Rhys ducked, and a large splash of ooze fell onto Sayd.

"What the -," Sayd screamed.

The three tried to contain it, dodging goop and ooze every time they dodged in front of it. Soon they were backed up against the wall, facing the blob. This was it. This was the end, Lacy thought. We're all about to drown in a flood of goop. Suddenly the blob jumped, pressing them flat against the wall. Breathlessly, the three were too squashed to speak. Mouths wide open in an effort to both breathe and cry for help, Portia dashed in to find them moments from becoming a part of the wall.

"What in Bruimhilda's name? I was only gone

for ten minutes."

"What is up with your hair". Sayd laughed

"What?" Portia ran to the washroom mirror and shrieked. Her hair was tangled, covered with leaves and looked like a rat's nest.

"Ok, can you fix your hair after getting this blob off of us?" Lacy scolded.

"Ugh, you're right," Portia said

She turned around and popped the cork off the beaker. Carefully she poured the glowing purple liquid onto the blob of flesh. A very loud belch erupted from the blob as the antidote seeps in. It slowly started to melt off them and become a tan liquid on the floor. Free, Rhys laughed hysterically.

"What's so funny?". Lacy snorted.

"It's funny because how is that supposed to go back to being a human." Rhys pointed to the liquid.

All of a sudden a hand started to form in the weird puddle of fluid.

"I guess we just wait until it goes back to being a student," Portia shrugged.

After a couple of minutes, a short blonde-haired boy flowed out of the puddle with a shocked look on his face.

"Um, you fell. Are you alright?" Lacy hedged.

"I fell. Is that why I'm on the floor?" He scratched his head and tried to get up but slipped on water that was on the ground and hit his head on the floor.

"Oh crap!" Rhys exclaimed.

The washroom door burst open.

"What's going on here?" The principal yelled as he and two teachers rushed inside.

"What happened to the boy?" One of the teachers asked.

"He just slipped on some water,". Portia said. "We rushed in to come to help him but he won't wake up."

"Oh really, he just happened to slip."

"Well, this is a washroom. And there is a large puddle of water here," Rhys said. "We assumed he slipped."

"You know what, you four, in detention right now!". The principal says.

"Not again."

Chapter 23

"Since when did the school make detention after school," Sayd groaned. "Isn't that cruel and unusual punishment?"

"Shhhh," the teacher hushed.

"I heard that too many people were getting detention, so now there's an after-school one too," Lacy whispered.

They weren't alone in detention. There were several other students scattered around minding their own business. Sayd and Lacy were sitting in front of Rhys, and Portia was on the other side of the room.

"Hey, aren't those guys on the basketball team." Rhys leaned forward and pointed to the guys in front of Sayd and Lacy.

"I think so. I'm pretty sure the one on the left is really good," Lacy said.

"What do you think they did?" Rhys questioned.

"Hey. Psst." Lacy leaned forward and tapped the one on the right.

He turned around with a raised eyebrow.

"Why are you guys in detention?" Sayd asked.

The one on the left turned to see what was going on. "We bounced a basketball off the trophy case and it broke. Now we have detention and are benched for the next two games."

"What did you guys do?" The one on the left asked.

"We apparently made a boy slip on water in the washroom," Lacy rolled her eyes. "All we did was try and help him.

"Wait, why were you in the boy's washroom."

"Long story."

The two boys turn around and continue to whisper back and forth between themselves. Twenty minutes later, the teacher monitoring detention left to grab something from the printer. Once the teacher was out the door, Portia stormed to the three and sat on the empty chair beside Rhys.

"You will not believe what I heard the students around me whispering," Portia stressed.

"What happened?" Lacy questioned.

"They were talking about how the history teacher is an ogre. Do you guys understand how bad this is?"

"We need to do something fast," Lacy said seriously.

Portia heard the teacher coming back and ran to her original seat, mouthing, we'll talk later.

Detention was finally over. The four waited until the next day to start their search. During lunch, the four headed back to their way to the lair to figure out what to do about this ogre. Rhys, Lacy and Sayd were panicking because they have no clue how to handle this ogre. Meanwhile, Portia is trying to devise a plan that would work. Somewhere, she had a scroll that explained how to trap an ogre, and she could not seem to concentrate with those three babbling.

"You guys have to stop panicking. I can't think," Portia scolded.

"What do you mean by stop panicking? I hate ogres!" Rhys exclaimed. "If we don't come up with a plan soon, we're gonna have a lot more work to do."

"You're right we are working with an ogre here, so let's make a plan," Sayd urged.

"Ok, um we'll need some ogre traps," Lacy said.

"Duh," Sayd snorted. "And you happen to have a few in your back pocket?"

"There must be some around here. We were fully equipped by the Ministry."

Sayd and Lacy started looking in the bags they packed full of equipment. Rhys and Portia scrambled around looking in every drawer, closet and niche. Sayd found a bag with lighting lances, and Portia found the cupboard that had the ogre traps. They planned to split up and have Sayd and Lacy go look in every room in the west wing, while Portia and Rhys searched the East wing.

"If you guys find him, don't wait for us. Do what you need to do and bring him to the lair," Portia said.

"Alright," Lacy mumbled while putting a couple of lances in her backpack.

Rhys and Portia walked off to start their search. A few seconds later, the others followed. Both pairs were doing the same thing. Looking in every class, the washrooms, the cafeteria, and the offices without finding a thing. After twenty minutes of searching, Portia and Rhys wandered back to the lair to think.

"Where could he possibly be?" Rhys threw up his hands in frustration. "Should we have even trusted what those kids were saying in detention?"

"I don't know anymore," Portia flopped down onto the couch. "Maybe Lacy and Sayd found something."

Almost on cue, Lacy and Sayd ran in.

"Did you guys find anything?"

"No, we were hoping you guys did," Sayd breathed.

"Let's just go outside and get some fresh air, and maybe we'll think of something," Lacy suggested. "There's a lovely thunderstorm moving in."

The four went outside and sat on the bench near the front entrance of the school, trying to come up with a plan. They saw a couple of girls in front of them and overheard them talking about the history teacher. They all immediately start eavesdropping to see if they will spill some information on him.

"I got a sixty percent on my essay! He has to hate me because I thought it was so good," one of the students said.

"I think he was being generous with that sixty, your essay was garbage." The other laughed.

"What do you mean it was garbage?"

"Well, you didn't follow the format and it was half the amount of words he asked for," the second girl explained.

"Guys stop, if you both paid attention in class, you would realize that he's actually a really good teacher." A different girl scolded.

The four looked at each other, confused because the boys in detention had said he was an ogre.

"Someone go ask one of them if he's an ogre," Portia said.

"Not it."

"Not it."

"Ugh, why me?" Lacy mumbled.

Lacy got up and walked toward the girl. She tapped one of them on the shoulder. All three of the girls turn around.

"Hey, I just overheard you guys talking about the history teacher, and a little while ago I also overheard that he was an ogre. Do you guys know if that's true?"

"Oh my gosh, he could never. He's a sweetheart, I can't believe someone called him an ogre." The girl who had been defending him earlier said.

"Same," Lacy laughs nervously. "I'm glad because I have him next semester. I'll see you guys around."

Lacy walked back to the group and plopped down on the bench.

"How'd it go," Portia asked.

"They couldn't even believe that I put 'history teacher' and 'ogre' in the same sentence. Apparently the guys a 'sweetheart' and those students in detention lied."

Defeat and relief crossed their features because, although they didn't have to deal with an ogre, they had wasted their entire lunch for nothing.

Chapter 24

While the magical barrier between the two groups had come down, the gulf between the conflicting theories remained.   Lacy and Portia decided to stake out the strange room on the second floor and didn't bother telling the other two their plans. Sooner or later, the Science Teacher would return here, and when he did, the others would follow. This time Portia decided to hit them with a tracking hex so that they could follow their movements around the school using the specially equipped crystal ball the Ministry had provided.

"Do you think they'll notice when you hex

them?" Lacy asked.

"I doubt these humans could tell the difference between a hex and a love spell," Portia replied. "Besides, I can be very subtle. I was top of my class in that course."

"Congratulations," Lacy cried. "It's good to be rewarded for your hard work."

Portia grunted. "If anyone was going to beat me for top of our year, I'm glad it was you."

"I do have to admit I had a lot of tutors," Lacy sighed. "I spent so much time in classrooms that I wasn't able to participate in school activities."

"I didn't know that."

Lacy shrugged. "Who notices the lone werewolf in a school full of witches, mummies and vampires?"

Portia wanted to say something but she knew it was true. No one made much of an effort to get to know the ghosts, ghouls or the one werewolf at the Academy. Despite all the changes over the last decade, everyone was still class conscious at the Academy.

"Hey!" Lacy hissed. "Is that him?"

Sure enough, the Science Teacher was trundling down the hallway with his arms full of boxes. As he came up to the small room, he leaned the boxes against the door while trying to fish his keys from his pocket.

"Could you to girls give me a hand?"

Startled, the two exchanged looks, wondering if he was talking to them. And then, realizing he had, they rushed forward to help.

"Here, take this one," he handed a box to

Portia. "Be careful with this one, it's heavy."

Werewolves were incredibly strong. What was heavy to a human weighed no more than a feather to a werewolf. Still, Lacy carried the box gingerly. His hands now free, the Science Teacher fished out his keys from a pocket and unlocked the doors.

"Just set the boxes down on the potting table there," the Science Teacher instructed.

"What is this place?" Lacy asked.

"It's a greenhouse," he explained – something teachers were always doing. "You use it for indoor plants or to start seedlings ahead of the growing season."

How could this be a greenhouse, Portia thought. "Isn't it too bright in here? I mean, won't all this sunlight burn the plants?"

"No," the Science Teacher laughed. "While there are shade plants, most plants love light and warmth."

"What do you do in here?" Lacy leaned in to watch over his shoulder.

"I'm conducting an experiment," he replied. "Here, let me show you."

With the girls watching he opened the first box and unloaded four bean sprouts, each in their own pot.

"Now, for an experiment to work, you need a control group – something to compare your experimental group to so you can test your hypothesis."

"Hypotomus?" Lacy asked through a giggle.

"Hypothesis," the Science Teacher corrected, switching to full teacher mode. "It's a theory you hope to prove. In this case, I hope to prove my latest formula for my green fertilizer is better or just as effective as the more environmentally harmful commercial fertilizers."

"And what will your new fertilizer do?" Portia still hoped it would connect up to the Abalaxia epidemic.

"Cure world hunger," he laughed. "And if not that, help take some of the harmful phosphates and nitrates from our waterways and leave you kids a cleaner and a safer world."

"And how do these four cuties help you do that?" Lacy asked, genuinely interested.

"Well," the Science Teacher pointed. "These two here I will let grow naturally. They will be my control group. This one I will treat with the commercial fertilizer, and this one with my own formula. Now, if these two outperform these two – that is, grow bigger and produce more beans – that will prove that fertilizer helps plants grow."

"I see," Lacy nodded. "And if this one grows better than this one it will mean your formula worked. But if this one grows bigger, it means it didn't."

"Precisely," he beamed. "Would you like to help me set up the experiment?"

"Very much," Lacy said. "You know I have a plant named Fig at home."

"Is it a fig tree?"

"I'm not sure what type of plant he is," Lacy admitted. "But he looks like a Fig to me, so that's what I named him."

"Have a bit of a green thumb do you?" The

Science Teacher teased.

"Oh," Lacy looked at her thumbs. "I hope not!"

"It just means you are good at raising plants."

"Oh," Lacy beamed. "Yes, I love growing things. I was always digging in my granny's garden when I was a pup."

While Portia stewed in the corner, disappointed that their suspect and their lead had not panned out, Lacy stood at the Science Teacher's elbow helping out. First, they labelled the four pots, two as the control group with a tape reading 'no fertilizer', one with 'commercial fertilizer', and one with 'green fertilizer'. Next Lacy helped him mix small amounts of fertilizer with water. These they poured into the two pots to be fertilized and set the four bean sprouts on a shelf near the window.

"I don't think it's working," Lacy said, leaning over one of the pots.

The Science Teacher laughed. "The lifecycle of a bean plant is several months from sprout to harvest. We won't know if our experiment worked for several weeks now."

"Maybe Portia could help," Lacy suggested hopefully.

Portia put a finger to her lips and began to gesture wildly behind the Science Teacher's back.

"She's welcome to help out," he said, "but I'm afraid there's nothing much for us to do now except wait."

"In that case," Lacy said, "do you think I could borrow a bit of that fertilizer? Fig doesn't seem to be doing well lately, and it might perk him up."

"I don't see why not," he agreed. "Let me see if

I have a jar around her we can use and I will pour you some."

The Science Teacher rooted around his boxes and bags until he found an empty baby food jar. He poured a small measure of the liquid fertilizer inside and securely closed the lid before handing it back to Lacy.

"Now," he instructed. "Mix a quarter of this with water and stir it well. You only need to fertilize once every month or two if you don't see much improvement. But be careful not to over-fertilize. Keep an eye out for signs of burnt leaves – leaves turning yellow and dying."

"I will," Lacy promised. "And thank you."

Portia pulled Lacy out of the greenhouse before she found another chore for them. Now that they had eliminated their suspect, the group only had one left – the Chaplain who was being followed by Rhys and Sayd.

"We are out of luck," Portia sighed. "I don't think their suspect is any better than ours, so that means we are absolutely nowhere on our case."

"I think it's nice he's trying to feed all those hungry people," Lacy hedged. "And I like him. He's okay, for a human that is."

The girls turned the corner near the main staircase when they ran into a group of boys. One of them stepped out of the pack. "Hey, Lacy, did you hear what happened to the security guard?"

"No, what?"

"Allan was swimming in the school pool when a spontaneous black hole opened up on the bottom. Now he's being forced to play the xylophone for these aliens on the other side of the dimensional rift."

"That's not what happened," a second boy objected. "He was playing lead kazoo for a techno band when Ben fell on him. Now he thinks he's Sting, and when he broke into Sting's mansion he got arrested."

"That wasn't Allan," the first boy retorted. "That was Ben."

"No, it wasn't!" A third added. "That was Jacob. Ben is the one who got eaten by goats while singing opera in Ghana."

While the boys argued the merits of each story, the girls slipped away and headed back to their lair. Maybe Rhys and Sayd had a more productive day.

Chapter 25

"You two and your stories," Portia complained as she threw herself onto the couch. "Everyone knows that extra-dimensional aliens don't like xylophones."

"What are you talking about?" Sayd laughed.

"We were up in the greenhouse talking to the Science Teacher and on our way here we ran into a group of boys," Portia sighed. "And they were telling the wildest tales that I know originated with you two."

"Wait," Rhys said, "you talked to the Science Teacher?"

"Oh, we've eliminated him as a suspect," Portia waved. "It's those crazy stories that have me worried."

"What about the Science Teacher?" Rhys insisted.

"I would kind of like to hear about these stories," Sayd teased.

"That can wait," Rhys said. "We have a mission

to finish, and an important one."

"Oh, alright then," Portia relented. "So we went up to stake out that little room, which turns out to be a greenhouse."

"That's a greenhouse," Sayd scoffed. "With all that sunshine?"

"Yep!" Lacy nodded. "And he's working on this really wild experiment so he can feed all the hungry without poisoning the world. Isn't that amazing?"

"Oh, yeah, it's special," Sayd snickered. "So how did you find all this out?"

"As I said," Portia continued. "We planned to stake it out and zap anyone who came to see him with a tracking hex. Only things didn't work out that way. When he came up his arms were so full of boxes he couldn't open the door."

"And so he asked us to help out," Lacy shrugged. "And we carried the boxes right inside. Smart, huh?"

"Oh, it's something alright," Rhys laughed. "Getting roped into helping out the person you're staking out is straight out of the detective's handbook."

"If it isn't, it should be," Lacy said. "If we didn't get in there today it could have taken us weeks to learn everything we learned today."

"Besides," Portia sneered, "what did you two do today? Another rousing game of Spiders and Bats?"

"We were going to stake out the Chaplain's office," Rhys said. "But she's not in today."

"The girls are right," Sayd said. "They did

prove that Portia and I were wrong to suspect the Science Teacher. Tell us what you discovered?"

"Well, it's pretty much as we've already said," Portia flopped further into the cushions of the couch.

"He's not brewing Abalaxia," Lacy said. "He's trying to invent a new kind of fertilizer. Oh, and he taught us all about a thing called an experiment. First, you get four bean sprouts – only they're not magical. Two you ignore, and one you give a fertilizer you know that works, and the last one you give your potion."

"So, it's magic?" Rhys asked.

"No," Lacy shook her head. "You're not allowed to use magic. I asked if Portia could help his plants grow and he laughed."

"So, what happened with the experiment?" Sayd asked.

"Oh, we won't know for absolutely weeks and weeks because it takes Human plants forever to grow."

"No wonder so many humans are hungry in this world," Rhys tsked. "Imagine having to take weeks to grow your food. I'd starve before I had enough mouldy grain for a decent loaf of bread."

"Well," Lacy sighed, "at least he gave me some of the fertilizer for Fig so I can do an experiment of my own."

"There's no way you're feeding it to that monstrosity," Rhys warned.

"Don't worry," Lacy giggled, "he wrote me out the instructions on how to use it."

Unfortunately, the Science Teacher wrote the instructions in green ink, and like all werewolves, Lacy was red-green colour blind. Unable to read what was on the page, she shrugged and dumped the whole jar into Fig's pot.

"Well," Lacy announced, "I'm going to bed. It's been a long day."

"Good night," the others called.

Well after midnight, when the four youths were struggling with their dreams, something strange overtook Fig. It started in its roots, which were swollen and pulsing.

"Tummy ache," it complained to the Mixmaster.

"Let me whip you up a ginger and arsenic tonic," the appliance offered.

Suddenly, an overgrown vine shot across the counter and knocked the Mixmaster from its perch. On the floor on its side, the Mixmaster scolded. "If you did not want a tonic, you merely had to say so. Violence will never get you anywhere."

Violent growth spurts were another matter altogether. They not only got Fig somewhere, but they also got it everywhere. Soon the Mixmaster and his friends were backed into a corner of the kitchen, fighting for their lives against a jungle of vines and shoots.

"I believe we have been here before," the grandfather clock intoned. "Facing certain doom in the face of a vegetable revolution."

"Have no fear, my friends," the Mixmaster called valiantly. "We shall prevail, and if not, we have died defending our masters and our homes."

"I'm too young to die," the Easy-Bake Oven

wailed.

"You were born in the '70s," the phonograph snorted. "You're an antique."

"Look who's talking," the Easy-Bake oven retorted. "Your warranty ran out while Bruimhilda was crafting her first spell."

"Gentlemen," the Mixmaster said, "and lady, we must stand united in this time of crisis."

"That's easy for you to say," the digital clock spat springs. "You're leading from the rear again."

"I am supplying vital logistical support in this our most critical battle."

Meanwhile, the four youths slept on oblivious to the drama unfolding beyond their bedroom doors. Adjusting to sleeping all night and being awake all day was beginning to wear on their systems. After tossing and turning for half the night, they had fallen into a deep slumber that would leave them more exhausted in the morning. Lately, Portia was beginning to sleep through the chanting of her grandfather clock and had been late for class twice this week.

This morning was no exception. She rolled over and suddenly realized she had not heard the alarm clock this morning.

"Lacy!" Portia called. "Lacy, did you muzzle the grandfather clock last night?"

"Why would I muzzle the grandfather clock?" Lacy complained. "You're the one that has problems getting up in the morning. If you trained yourself by having twenty naps, like I do, you wouldn't have problems sleeping at night."

"That's funny," Portia said. "Something must be

wrong."

"Don't look at me," Lucy yawned. "I'm going to have a nap before I get dressed."

Sighing and groaning, Portia struggled out of bed. Groggily she stumbled to the door, blinking bleary-eyed at the gathering daylight. At the door, she pushed and it pushed back, sending her sprawling onto the floor.

"By Merlin's beard!" She cursed. "Lacy, come help me with the door."

"What's wrong with the door?"

"It's stuck," Portia said. "Either that or the boys have barricaded us in our room. Now, come help me."

"They're immature enough to do it," Lucy yawned.

But it was not the boys who had barricaded them in their room. At that moment they were struggling to exit their own bedroom. Sayd tried stepping through the door to see what was blocking it and something threw him back into the room and sent him flying head-over-heels across the room.

"What was that?" Rhys asked. "Some kind of magical barrier?"

"I don't think so," Sayd groaned. "It tasted a little woody to me."

"Come give me a hand and we'll brute force our way out."

In the end, the boys broke the door down with a little help from whatever was on the other side. At the same moment, Portia blasted their door out of existence with a hex. The four stood staring across a field of withering vines, standing in their doorways unable to move any further into the living room.

"Lacy!" The three snapped.

She shrugged. "Well, at least we know our lair is secure."

Chapter 26

The Exorcist frowned. Fitting in at this school was proving more difficult than he had anticipated. For one, he had trouble relating to teenagers, human or otherwise. And finally, his quest for information was uncovering a host of bizarre stories. Apparently, a number of students were missing, which he already had anticipated given his client's activities. Still, being eaten by a hoard of mice while fleeing from a butterfly was too fantastical in any world. And who could play the bongos so fast that they lit themselves on fire?

Perhaps the Abalaxia was affecting these humans in ways no one knew. Something was affecting their reasoning. If he heard one more story about flying toads or sinkholes, the Exorcist would see if he could banish a human to the seventh plane of Hell. The Tara person, however, sounded interesting. So did this Karlee person, the flying nun who collided with a 747 while trying to rescue orphans.

"Perhaps." The Exorcist thought, "none of these kids really existed. Half of these tales sounded like the plot from one of those binge videos."

He looked down and consulted the list of students provided to him from his contact on the school staff. The Exorcist was looking for a girl named Nelly.

"Hello my children," he greeted a group of girls who were hanging around in one of the stairwells. "Do any of you know a girl named Nelly?"

"Which one?" A girl asked. "The one with the pigtails and braces, or the one that ran away with the gypsy and became the Gypsy Queen?"

"Gypsy Queen?" The Exorcist struggled to keep his voice even.

"Yeah," a second girl said. "You know, the girl from that song:

> Sign of the Gypsy Queen
> Sign of the girl that glows…"

"I'm not quite sure."

Portia saw the Exorcist down below and pulled the others back through the door with her. She was not fooled by that phony priest's getup, and neither was any of her companions. You did not grow up in the Otherworld without being able to spot the biggest bogeyman from that world.

"There he is again," she complained.

"Quick," Rhys urged. "We'll cut around outside and come in from the gym door."

"Did you notice he's working off some kind of list?" Sayd asked.

"I wonder if our names are on it," Lacy said.

"I could easily find out," Sayd suggested.

"No," Portia warned. "You stay away from that Exorcist. Don't forget that he can sense your presence."

"Yeah," Sayd objected, "but I'll just -."

"You'll just nothing," Rhys snapped. "Someone is spending a lot of silver if they sent a heavy hitter to take us out. This must be a lot bigger than either we or the Ministry of Magical Artefacts thought."

And that was food for thought for all of them. A simple recovery of stolen potions was blowing up in their faces, and the repercussions could affect both worlds for decades to come.

"Well," Lacy said thoughtfully, "what's so different about Abalaxia when it's used by humans?"

"Simple," Portia said. "They turn into monsters."

"I see what Lacy is getting at," Sayd said. "Who would want monsters? What are they used for?"

"We do not use monster labour in any of our businesses!" Rhys snapped.

"Oh," Lacy beamed. "I heard about that. There was a big scandal about it that upset the troll and orc unions. Remember, it was all over the crystal balls for weeks, and even the High Council had to issue a statement."

"Yeah," Portia said. "I remember. And some owner from an obscure company was arrested, wasn't he."

"Well," Lacy sighed, "it was just a thought. I guess that didn't amount to anything."

"Let's hurry," Rhys urged, "we need to get in behind that priest if we are going to do any investigating before class."

His three companions nodded and picked up their pace. The last time they had seen the Exorcist he was talking to a group of girls near the middle stairs closest to the upstairs washrooms. They were racing across the front of the school, hoping to slip in through the doors by the gym and cross the first floor before he crossed the second. In this manner, they hoped to stay one step ahead of him and stay under the radar. The problem with this plan was that they never knew where he was heading, and could accidentally run into him at any moment. And this is exactly what happened.

Rhys looked up and saw the black cassock from a distance. It was in the doorway nearest the student parking lot, and he reversed direction. "He beat us here somehow. Quickly, let's make our way to the front doors."

Inside, the Exorcist paused to talk to a mixed group of students. "Hello, my children. You wouldn't possibly be able to help me, would you?"

"Sure thing, Father."

"You wouldn't happen to know a student named Tara by any chance?" He asked.

"Is she the one who was eating the pizza when the black hole opened up in its middle?" One of the girls asked, "or is she the one who drowned in the pot of melted cheese?"

"I'm pretty sure that was Elliot," a boy cut in. "Tara got eaten by the possessed car."

"You got it all wrong both of you," a third

student broke in. "Ranah was the one who got eaten by the car. Tara tripped over a chair and fell into that crack in the cafeteria. In fact, I hear they are mounting an expedition to save her. Coach is supposed to post a signup list by his door today. I was thinking I might join it."

"That sounds like fun," another boy said. "But what happened to Elliot?"

The Exorcist shook his head in disgust and walked away. Every time he asked about one of the students on his list he got the same babble of nonsense. The last time he was in the Human world he did not remember humans being so distracted. So far every student on his list proved to be missing, and unless he believed the crazy stories, no one knew where they had disappeared. Somewhere in this school were four Recovery Agents from the Ministry of Magical Artifacts and he was determined to find them, and find them quickly because he had no intention of staying in this loony bin any longer than necessary.

The bell rang to end the first lunch, sending the kids scrambling back to class. The Exorcist found a quiet corner where he could review his list of names, crossing out several names in angry frustration. He meant to use the brief period between the two lunch periods to figure out a different approach since all his earlier attempts had ended in failure. Perhaps rather than asking the students, he should approach some of the teachers. He would give it one more lunch period and if he made no progress, the Exorcist would spend some time in the teachers' lounge during the next couple of days.

Students streamed into the hall ahead of the bell for the second period, something they would never do in the Otherworld. The Exorcist stayed in his corner, giving it another five or ten minutes while the students settled in for lunch or returned to their classrooms. Once they had settled in he moved off into the atrium to scout out the groups of kids. Coming into the atrium he spotted a likely group hanging out beneath the main stairwell, a group who seemed to stick to themselves. Perhaps this would not prove the most fruitful hunting ground, and still, he felt he could not afford to leave any stone unturned.

"Excuse me, children," he drifted into the shadows beneath the stairs as silent as a breeze. "I was wondering if any of you might know a Jebediah?"

"Jebediah?" A girl spoke up. "Isn't there a Jebediah in our Art class?"

"No," a second girl nodded. "That's Jeremiah."

The Exorcist was hopeful. This was the first time he had stumbled upon a rational response so he decided to risk it. "Perhaps you know a Lacy?"

"Oh yes," the first girl brightened. "Everyone knows Lacy."

"We've known her for years," another girl lied. "Didn't she use to go to our grade school?"

"Oh, for sure," the first girl wanted everyone to think she knew Lacy the best. "Although she wasn't as popular in Grade school as she is now."

Frowning, the Exorcist crossed another two names off his list. Perhaps he had mistaken that first day.

Chapter 27

Constable O'Flannery was a newly minted School Resource officer and already a serious investigation had popped up on his patch. Some twenty students had disappeared from John Paul II Secondary School. Nervously, he exited his patrol car and headed inside to begin the initial interviews on a case that was bound to head straight to the Major Crimes Unit. How could it not? Twenty missing students and no one saying anything. He was good with kids, one of the reasons he was chosen for this duty, and he knew kids this age would rather die than be seen to be ratting on their friends.

Inside he headed straight into the office to speak with the receptionist. "Hello, I'm here to investigate the disappearance of some of your students. Is there someone here I can speak with?"

"The principal's office is straight back," the receptionist replied. "I believe he is in his office at the moment."

The Principal was hunched over his back desk, busily polishing an imagined scratch from one of the school trophies when a knock sounded at his door. He looked up with a start when he saw the police officer standing outside his office.

"Hello, can I help you?"

"Yes," O'Flannery said. "I'm here to investigate the disappearance of some of your students. I was wondering if there was someplace I could set up to do some student interviews."

"Oh, yes," the Principal nodded. "We do have an office for the School Resource office. Let me show you where it is. Any students you need to see, you can have our receptionist call them down to the office over the intercom."

"I appreciate the cooperation."

Soon he was ensconced in his new office, setting up his notepads and pens in anticipation of his first interview. He had chosen to interview some of the friends of one of the athletes from the girls' basketball team, who had disappeared during a trip down into the States to tour some of the big ten colleges.

Stepping out into the main office, he called, "can you please send in the first student."

His first interviewee was a teammate of the missing girl. From the moment she walked in and threw herself into the chair, sitting sprawled over one of its arms, O'Flannery knew this would be a difficult session.

"Thank you for coming in," he said. "I wanted to ask you about one of your friends, a Sandra Owens. Do you know where she is?"

"Oh her," the student sneered. "She's on a school trip down into the States to tour some of the Big Ten colleges. I don't know why they picked her and not me, I'm by far a better power forward than she is. I've scored thirty-three more rebounds this season than she did, and have been first string since my first year."

"I see," O'Flannery nodded. "Well, thank you for your time."

Most of his interviews about the missing athletes went along a similar vein. Everyone claimed they had gone on a school trip to tour some colleges, and many were bitter that they had not gotten picked to go. There was another group of interviews about a select group of students not associated with school athletics that went off on bizarre tangents that left the officer shaking his head. What did he do with these? Should he even write any of this up, or would he be laughed off the force if he did?

One particular interview came to mind. The student in question was listed as a Maybelline Evans but insisted on being called Pat. She wore nondescript clothes that did not come close to a uniform, something the office might have referred to as in the Goth style but suspected it had a strong Anime influence. She plopped down into the chair, got up and spun it around, and sat leaning forwards against its back.

"I thought you'd get around to me eventually," she said, "cause I know all about the missing students and the security guard. I was there when some of it happened."

"You do?" O'Flannery nodded, "and you were?"

"Go ahead," Pat challenged, "give me a name and I will tell you what happened."

"How about the security guard," O'Flannery asked, "Do you know what happened to him?"

"I've heard several stories myself," Pat leaned back, "but the real 4-1-1 is that he retired and moved to Ghana to take up a career teaching Hyenas to dance. I know, because he told me himself the day he left. If you don't believe me, you can ask Sayd, he was there too."

"And how about Ben?"

"Oh, nothing mysterious about that," Pat snorted. "He was run over by a couple of guys on skateboards and hit his head. Now he thinks he's Ironman and spends all his time in the garage trying to invent a power suit. In between, he plays kazoo with a local band."

"Let me guess," O'Flannery said, "this Sayd can back you up."

"True dat."

"And Tara?"

"Oh, she got a job as a lifeguard in the Hospitality class. One day she fell into a pot of tomato soup and drowned. Ever since then," Pat assured the officer, "the Hospitality class has not been allowed to make tomato soup."

"And Ranah?"

"You remember the sinkhole out front. You know, the one they spent all night covering up so we could come to school the next day. Unfortunately, she tripped and fell into it and they actually buried her alive. If you stand at just the right place on the sidewalk, you can hear her tapping on a pipe."

"And Elliot?"

"Oh well," Pat sighed. "The crows caught him. It was all over the news when they dropped him as they were flying away and he got caught on that low flying plane. Do you know if they recovered his body yet?"

"I haven't heard anything," O'Flannery fought to keep from rolling his eyes. "How about Karlee?"

"Oh, she ran away with the circus and fell into a cannon."

"And Jacob?"

"Lost at sea in an orange rowboat," Pat nodded. "Got swept out to sea when he was fishing for walruses."

"And Nelly."

"Well, you remember how Rosanne Barr got into trouble because of her big mouth?" Pat looked up at the ceiling. "Nelly got her part for the new show."

"I thought they cancelled the reboot."

"Oh no, it's still on in reruns."

"Well Pat, thank you very much for your candour. I think that just about wraps things up."

Constable O'Flannery had sat through several other interviews that ran something along the same lines. Sighing in frustration, he gathered up his papers and placed them in his briefcase. Outside the door, he ran into the principal.

"Well sir," Constable O'Flannery said, "that's it for today. I'm sure others will be coming back to investigate further. We will need copies of any and all paperwork relating to this school trip most of these students were on."

"No problem," the Principal nodded. "I'll have my office manager make copies for you. You said only some of the students?"

"There's this group here," the constable handed over a list.

"Oh, those are the Pens of John Paul II."

"And what are these Pens of John Paul II?"

"An afterschool writing club," the Principal explained. "They meet here in the library unless it's in use, then they meet in the cafeteria, or maybe even the Jag room. Oh, and did you check the broom closet down the hall?"

"I don't think that will be necessary at this point," the constable said. "There are some silly stories circulating amongst the students about their disappearance. They seem to be attributed to a student named Sayd. Harmless, I guess, but if any of them get back to the families it could be very upsetting. You might want to speak to him."

"I'll see to it right away."

When the two men said their goodbyes the Principal headed directly into his office, where he scribbled a quick note. A moment later, he left the office and headed off across the atrium, where he left it in the mailbox of the new priest.

Chapter 28

During their last meeting, the two had set up a dropbox to exchange information. Fortunately, the school had a convenient internal mail system that made it all the easier. The Exorcist headed towards the mailroom, seeking to distract himself from the frustration of his latest round of interviewing teachers and students. He found a note in his mailbox and recognized the handwriting right away. Not wanting to open it where prying eyes might see, he retreated across the atrium and entered the door to the left of the cafeteria that led up to his office.

Squeezing past the scissor lifts that were stored here, the Exorcist made his way up the stairs that led to a room overlooking the cafeteria. Some days he preferred to stay up here, looking down at the students below without being observed. He was learning much about the habits of human teenagers from watching them interact during breaks, although it was not helping him identify the Recovery agents.

"Let us see what we have here," he murmured as he took the note from his pocket and opened it. "Sayd, do you say. And his next class will be Math. I think I shall follow this Sayd and see what I can learn."

The Math classes were on the second floor. The Exorcist decided he would set himself up at one end of the hall, leaning up against the wall where he could see its entire length. From there he ought to be able to watch this student and see what direction he headed. But first, he would swing by the classroom and get a peek at this Sayd so he would know who he needed to follow. And one glance into the classroom and he not only knew which student he needed to follow, he recognize him for what he was – a poltergeist.

The Exorcist returned to his post at the end of the hall, thinking. Although he always came prepared to banish all types of creatures, getting rid of a poltergeist was notoriously difficult. And his presence here did not necessarily mean he was one of the Recovery agents. With their natural ability to travel between worlds, poltergeists were always popping up in the Human world, usually where they were least wanted. And to banish them one had to capture them in a circle of salt, not the easiest thing to do when dealing with a creature who could pass through solid materials and throw objects from hundreds of feet away.

"But you will be my Judas goat," the Exorcist murmured. "And if you are part of the team I seek, you will lead them all to me."

The bell rang and the students streamed into the hall, a great horde that not only made it difficult to see his quarry at the other end but made it almost impossible to follow him. There was nothing for it, he would have to move right away and risk being sighted by his quarry or give up the chase for the day. The Exorcist pushed his way into the throng, using his size and his cassock to clear a path. Already this Sayd had entered the hallway and was making his way towards the nearest stairs. No hope he would pause at the bathroom – lacking a body, poltergeist had no bodily functions or physical needs. He would be down amongst the students on the first floor well before the Exorcist could travel the length of the hall.

As he came up to the Chaplain's office, she came out to greet him. "Father, I'm glad I ran into you. I intended to introduce myself much sooner but haven't got the opportunity before now. I'm the Chaplain here."

"Nice to meet you, my child," the Exorcist seethed inside at the delay and yet had to maintain his cover. "How do you enjoy it here?"

"Oh," the Chaplain smiled, "the children are wonderful. We have the normal complement of issues, and a good dozen or two who come for counselling – but then, that's why we are here."

"It is indeed," the Exorcist nodded, turning to look up the hall. "And speaking of counsel, I believe I see a child I've been meaning to speak with. If you will excuse me, so nice to meet you. We will definitely talk at a later date."

"Certainly Father, and welcome to John Paul."

The delay had definitely allowed his quarry to slip away. Still, there was only so far he could go. Those stairs either led down to the atrium or outside, and if the poltergeist were meeting others, he was most likely in the atrium. The Exorcist quickened his pace in the thinning crowds and moved rapidly down the hallway. He would be downstairs soon enough, and once he got there he would decide on his next move.

Sayd had met up with Lacy on the stairs and continued by without stopping. "I'm being followed by the Exorcist. Don't stop. Keep going and find the others, then tell them to do their best to avoid me. I will meet you all back in the lair as soon as I can."

Lacy nodded imperceptibly and moved away as Sayd continued his way down to the first floor. He had no intention of losing his tail so soon, planning to take him on a bit of a wild goose chase to give the others time to get safely back to the lair. If his cover was compromised, the others would have to avoid him as much as possible until they came up with a plan to eliminate the exorcist. In the meantime, he paused at the bottom of the stairwell, listening to the conversation of the girls who sat there while he waited for the Exorcist to catch up with him. Sayd would let him see him interacting with a dozen different groups before he finally gave the hunter the slip and made his way back to their lair.

Fortune was on the side of the Exorcist. As he came up to the stairwell, he spotted his quarry at the bottom of the stairs. He paused on the second landing, pretending to catch his breath as he studied the companions of the poltergeist. The Exorcist did not recognize any of the girls talking to the ghost, most of them Philippian, and none of them on the list he had received from his contact on the school staff. This might only be a chance encounter, he thought, the poltergeist distracted as his kind so often were, or one or more of the group were agents themselves. The Exorcist doubted the latter was true.

Something had spooked his spook. Perhaps he had caught sight of the Exorcist's cassock in the corner of his eye, or perhaps he had merely felt eyes on him. Once again his quarry was on the move, and the Exorcist waited another minute before giving chase. The poltergeist led him down into the first-floor halls and off towards the bathrooms nearest the Tech hallway, where he stopped again to speak with another group of students – a group of boys who were cutting up at the entrance to the boys' washroom. Again the Exorcist gave them a brief once over, sure these too were not agents.

While he waited, the Exorcist began to think. He needed to find the perfect spot to set a trap for this poltergeist. Once he had the poltergeist in his grasp, it would be easy enough to lure the others into a foolish attempt to rescue him. They were young and inexperienced enough to fall for such a ploy, yet it really depended on the location and his options were rather limited in this crowded school.

His quarry was on the move again. The Exorcist allowed him a few steps head start and followed at a leisurely pace. The boy had to be heading outside because there were no other options. That is if he did not double back or head back up to the second floor. The Exorcist frowned. He was beginning to suspect the poltergeist was leading him on a merry little chase to nowhere. Poltergeists were like that, finding joy in irritating and pestering the living. And somehow the Exorcist suspected this one was worse than most. If he weren't, there was little hope that he had attracted the attention of the Academy or the Ministry. The Exorcist would have to keep that in mind in his future interactions.

Sure enough, the poltergeist headed up the stairs towards the second floor. The Exorcist followed, beginning to get winded. Energy was wasted on the young. They never seemed to know what to do with it, other than run around in circles. And the Exorcist was definitely being led in a circle. They were almost back to where the chase had started, travelling up the Art and ESL hallway back towards the second-story bathrooms. Such behaviour was normal, not only for a poltergeist but for human teenagers as well. Still, by this time, his quarry had to know he was being followed – these hallways were too empty for anything else.

Sayd turned the corner and moved halfway down towards the middle stairwell when suddenly he turned to wait for the Exorcist. As the man turned the corner, startled to see the poltergeist, Sayd waved goodbye and melted through the floor.

Chapter 29

Portia walked around the hallway deep in thought. This new twist with Sayd and the Exorcist was making it difficult for them to continue their investigation, and they were now nowhere with the Chaplain and the Science Teacher eliminated as suspects. Something Lacy had said stuck with her, no matter how hard Portia tried to shake it. If someone was intentionally turning Humans into monsters, and transporting them back to the Otherworld, the implications were too dark to contemplate. Why would anyone want so many monsters? It could not be for anything good, and Portia doubted it was to use as slave labour as Sayd had suggested. There had to be some other reason, and Portia had no idea what it could be.

Maybe the Ministry of Magical Artifacts should have sent a more experienced team of agents. High school or not, she and her team were making a hash of this investigation, and once again they were barely talking to each other. If something big did come down the pipeline, were they up to the task? Portia doubted it.

Ahead she spotted three students scuttling about in the shadows. What were they doing at school so late? Even the custodians had gone home for the night, and Portia had thought it was safe to go out for a stroll to escape the tense atmosphere back at the lair. Watching them from the distance, she slipped into the shadows.

Hidden in the darkness Portia slowly crept closer to spy on the three students. Something in the darkness was distracting their attention, and this allowed her to come closer than she would have normally attempted. From her new vantage point, she paused to watch and immediately regretted it. The thing that was distracting the three students was raw meat – of what or who she could not tell – and these creatures were currently feasting on it like a horde of rats at a carcass.

"Yum, yum," one of the beasts groaned. "Mine!"

A second jumped him, tearing a piece of meat from its hands. "Mine! It's mine!"

Leaving them to squabble over the meat, Portia crept back through the shadows. As soon as she had put enough distance between herself and them, she began to run back towards the library and their lair. They needed to grab their equipment and return as soon as possible. They would need three antidotes, maybe nets, and definitely shock sticks if they did not want to become those beasts' next meal. How the familiar distance seemed to stretch on when you were in a hurry Portia could not fathom? But today this short run back to the lair seemed to stretch on into eternity, and her legs felt like lead weights that had been welded to the floor.

Portia stumbled huffing into the lair to find the others hunched over a game board, once again playing Spiders and Bats. "Hurry! Huff, huff. Monsters."

Without waiting to see how they had reacted, Portia turned to search for her bag. It was already gearing up for a game of chase when she snagged it roughly by the drawstrings and yanked it to her side. "Not today. I've got no time for play. Spit out three antidotes right this second or I will roast you where you stand."

"What's the panic?" Rhys yawned.

"There are three monsters in the hallway and we need to capture them right this second," Portia snapped.

"Couldn't it wait until after our game?" Sayd suggested. "After all, we have all night."

"They are eating raw meat!" Portia spun, sending a hex towards her three companions that concussed with lightning over the game board. "Now get up off your lazy butts and gather your equipment."

"Three did you say?" Lacy asked as she scampered off for her pack.

"Three," Portia nodded. "And if they haven't turned already, they are a heartbeat away from transforming. Humans don't eat raw meat."

"Where would they find raw meat in the school?" Rhys wondered.

"That is a question, isn't it," Portia said. "And here's another, where will they find more when that runs out? I fancy we're the only source of meat left in the school at this time of night, don't you?"

Rhys and Sayd came off the couch and raced off to gather their shock sticks. Meat-eaters were no laughing matter, and this was no case of students calling a teacher an ogre. If Portia saw three of these creatures in the hallway, there very well might be more waiting out in the darkness. Suddenly darkness was no longer as friendly as it had once seemed.

The four met at the door, loaded down with equipment. Portia led the way out of the lair and into the atrium, taking a hard left at a full run towards the gym hallway. At the doors leading into the hallway, she came to a skidding halt.

"There they are!"

The four stared in horror. The three creatures were hanging halfway up the walls on either side, still chewing on raw meat as they turned at the sound of Portia's voice. One look at the hunters and they raced away, one climbing up to the ceiling in his haste to escape. The agents gave chase, skidding through the blood and scraps of meat that was left behind by the creatures' meal.

"I think we can assume they are fully transformed now," Rhys called as he surged ahead of the others.

As the four rounded the corner, the creatures came dashing along the ceiling back the way they had come. Spinning on a heel, the four gave chase back towards the atrium with Lacy now in the lead.

Portia sent a hex flying towards the creature, which only doubled their speed as they scuttled away.

"Try and drive them into the far hallway!" Sayd called. "If they get out into the open we'll never be able to find them."

Too late. As one, the three insectoids raced straight for the cafeteria. Once there they split up, each running along the walls towards a deeper pool of shadows. Moonlight spilled in through the window, interfering with the night vision of the hunters who followed. But no matter. Gathering his inner poltergeist, Sayd raced ahead, a hurricane wind that swept up everything in its path. Driven by this gale, the three creatures scuttled a breakneck speed towards the stage, where they quickly chewed a hole through the curtain and disappeared inside.

"Sayd and I will go flush them out from behind the stage," Rhys called. "You two go around and cut them off in the hallway."

Rhys leapt onto the stage in one bound, following in the wake of Sayd who was hot in pursuit. All was dark behind the stage, a big empty space with lots of cubbyholes to hide in, but Sayd was very familiar with this part of the school. He had been here on several occasions. Why, he could not remember. Only the layout remained in his mind. With Rhys's help, he got in behind the three creatures and began chasing them towards the music room and the hall beyond. The insectoids were quick, too quick for the nets the two carried but keeping ahead of these kept them moving out towards the hallway where the others waited.

Portia and Lacy arrived at the door of the Music

room when the first of the creatures burst through. With a well-cast net, Lacy managed to capture it before it could climb out of reach. As Portia struggled to pull an antidote from the pocket of her robe, two others burst out through the door. Rhys and Sayd managed to nab a second creature with a net as they joined the girls. The third scuttled off and disappeared around the corner as its mates struggled with the netting and the four agents.

"Hold its mouth open," Portia cried.

"What part is its mouth?" Lacy giggled.

"The part that's trying to bite you," Rhys suggested, turning to help Lacy hold down the first creature in the net.

Portia dashed in and poured the potion down its throat, already reaching for a second as her companions turned towards the second. Once the second potion was administered, the four waited only long enough for the creatures to grow quiescent before retrieving their nets and turning to give chase to the last monster.

"Where did it go?" Rhys asked as they spun around the corner.

"Check the doors!" Portia suggested.

The four raced up and down the hallway, checking each door and finding them locked. There was no place for the creature to go, and yet it had disappeared. Sayd even dashed through each of the rooms beyond the locked doors and found them empty.

"There could only be one solution," Lacy determined. "If it's not here, it has to be in the Otherworld."

"You mean an inter-dimensional portal?" Rhys breathed.

"Lacy is right," Portia sighed. "What other solution is there? Face it, someone from back home is collecting monsters. Abalaxia and its side effects must be known to our culprit, and bringing it here was deliberate."

Chapter 30

The time was ripe, as they say. The Exorcist knew the route from his desk to the door and back and could walk it blindfolded. Now, all he needed was to lure the poltergeist into his office. And if that meant playing another game of bop-the-mole with the ghost, so be it. Once he had that one in his trap, the others would follow, falling like dominoes. The Exorcist knew their type. They would not leave a friend behind no matter what the cost and that was the weakness he hoped to exploit.

The Exorcist crept down the stairs and out into the atrium. He was never sure where that annoying ghost went to after their encounters, nor could he predict where he would run into him.

"So I shall wander and see what may come," the Exorcist muttered.

Not having a destination in mind, the Exorcist headed in the first direction he saw. This led him down towards the Tech hallway with only one way to go – up to the second floor. He paused at the bathrooms, half expecting the poltergeist to pop up here as he had so many times in the last couple of days. Nothing. Now that he was actively seeking the poltergeist, the contrary being was hiding.

In the stairwell two voices caused him to pause immediately inside the door.

"If we've told you once," Portia seethed, "we've told you a million times. You can't wander off on your own. Every time you do, you put our mission in jeopardy, what with sticking your head into places it doesn't belong and causing localized wind storms."

"Sometimes I just need a little space," Sayd said. "Besides, you never believe anything I say, so I have to investigate everything myself."

"That's because the things you say never make any sense," Portia sighed. "Besides, you forget half of what you mean to say. If you'd bring one of us with you, we could explain things to the others."

"You three don't listen," Sayd snapped. "I told you all about the thing with the what-do-you-call-it, and how I found the place."
"You see," Portia threw up her hands, exasperated. "What was the thing, or the what-do-you-call-it?"

"No I don't," Sayd retorted. "So you hear? Because I am speaking Salem English!"

"If you were," Portia laughed, "we wouldn't be having this conversation."

"There's no talking to you."

Sayd stormed off, rattling the windows and flicking posters off the wall. The Exorcist stepped quietly through the doors and swiftly raced to the other stairway to cut the poltergeist off.   When he needed to the Exorcist could move almost as rapidly as those he chased, and the poltergeist was in no hurry.   And so, the Exorcist came up onto the second floor ahead of Sayd and positioned himself where he could watch the poltergeist as he passed by without being seen.

At the top of the hallway, he met up with Lacy and the two disappeared into the drafting class. "So," the Exorcist thought, "I was right about one of your colleagues.   The little werewolf is a Recovery agent."

It struck him odd that the Ministry would send two individuals so young. Field agents usually had years of training, some living amongst humans for so long they were almost indistinguishable.   These two stuck out like a lighthouse on a clear night, visible for miles. And that thought gave him pause.

"Could these two and their companions be bait?" The Exorcist wondered. "And if so, who was the target?"

There was an outside chance that the answer was himself.   He had heard of such things, sting operations set up to lure an exorcist to his doom. It was an urban legend that suddenly held a lot of credence until the bell rang and the kids spilled out into the hall. The poltergeist didn't even wait for the door to open. He walked right through in and into the hall without breaking stride, leaving his companion to cover for his blunder.

Sayd led his stalker down into the atrium, where he met a group of five or six boys. Any one of them could be another Recovery agent, but there was no way for the Exorcist to tell from this distance. Nor could he chance to come any closer, not without alerting his target. Instead, he stood at the edge of the crowd, waiting to see where this group of boys would lead him.

Two of the six broke off from the group and went their separate ways. The other four entered the hall leading to the Tech hallway, pausing briefly by the bathrooms to flirt with some girls. Here, it was difficult to tell the humans from the non-humans. The two groups were perfectly blended, and if the Exorcist did not know the poltergeist for what he was, he would never have been able to pick Sayd out from the crowd. Finally, these agents were displaying a bit of spycraft.

These human classes went on forever. The Exorcist was tempted to retire to his office but he needed to study the poltergeist's routing if he was to spring his trap. And because these classes tended to be so long, the students ofter wandered. There was more than an outside chance this Sayd would slip out of class. It was what his kind did best, able as they were to slip through a wall and back again without notice.

The Exorcist was beginning to drowse when Sayd stepped out of a locker. "Now where are you going?" The Exorcist wondered.

Unseen, he watched as his prey drifted off towards the far stairs and the second floor. Once he had moved through the doors, the Exorcist began to follow. The hallway beyond the stairs was long enough that he could let his prey clear the stairwell before making his own ascent. There was only one direction Sayd could go. It was not until he reached the second turn that the hallway diverged, one fork continuing on to the balcony over the atrium, the second turning towards a second stairway and the bathrooms.

As long as he reached the corner in time, the Exorcist figured he could still arrive soon enough to see which way the ghost boy was heading. And as luck would have it, Sayd turned left towards the second-floor bathrooms, still too engrossed in his anger to notice who was following.

When Sayd did not enter this common hangout, the Exorcist was startled enough to mutter, "what are you up to?"

Waiting at the corner just out of sight, the Exorcist followed the boy with his eyes as he meandered down the hall. Three-quarters of the way along the boy stopped, looked up and down the corridor, and then melted into the floor. Caught by surprise, the Exorcist bolted from his perch on the wall and darted towards the stairs. He raced down the stairs, hoping to reach the atrium before the poltergeist disappeared.

And when he arrived, positioning himself between the boy and his class, there was no sign of the poltergeist.

"Where could you have gotten to?" The Exorcist walked towards the office and peeked inside without seeing any sign of the poltergeist.

Where could he have gone to? Puzzled, the Exorcist kept on passed the office until he came to the next set of doors, which led to the library. It was the only other place he could have gone, but why he would go to the library was beyond the Exorcist.

Inside, he saw several students sitting at lonely tables, quietly working away at assignments. One student sat way in a corner, reading a book, and the librarian was pushing a cart amongst the shelves as she returned errant books to their places. Everywhere he looked there was no sign of the poltergeist. He had disappeared. But no matter, the traps were set, and sooner or later he would fall into one.

Chapter 31

The Exorcist was back, Sayd thought. He had mentioned it to the others and met a lukewarm response, so lukewarm that the poltergeist was convinced that they did not believe him. There was no doubt about it in his mind, his cover had been blown and the Exorcist was actively hunting him. And if that was the case, Sayd decided, there was only one thing to do about it. It was time to turn the tables. He would hunt the hunter, and no one was better suited for the task than a poltergeist.

Sayd glanced back to make sure the Exorcist was still there and then quickly turned a corner. Once out of sight, he stepped through the wall and into an empty classroom. He had checked before taking this action, not able to afford the screams and cries of alarm that happened every time he stepped into an occupied classroom. Now he waited.

Poking his head back through the wall so that

only his eyes were visible, Portia watched for the Exorcist. Soon enough he came strolling around the corner, pausing as he looked back and forth before deciding to continue towards the stairs leading up to the second floor. Now it was Sayd's turn to wait for his quarry to get ahead of him, the hunted becoming the hunter. With poltergeists, such things came naturally. As he sensed his prey move up the stairs, Sayd stepped out of the wall and began to follow.

"How do you like those mushrooms?" Sayd snickered. "Keep looking, my Exorcist. I'm sure your quarry is a few steps ahead of you. Perhaps around that corner, or maybe the next."

Sayd paused inside the doors of the stairway, knowing that his prey had stopped in the upstairs hallway to figure out his next move. Which way do you think I've gone? Should I drift up and give you a peek? The thought tickled Sayd and almost he was tempted to try exactly that, only restraining himself with the knowledge that if he did he would never be able to follow the Exorcist back to his lair. Better to wait and let the poor fellow lead the way, so Sayd set himself to learn some patience.

Despite the humour in the situation, tailing a suspect was rather boring. Twice Sayd almost became distracted by the doings of other students as he followed the Exorcist through the halls. He couldn't resist popping a balloon near the balcony overlooking the atrium, and he had to sink through a wall when the noise attracted the attention of his target. Sometimes being a poltergeist had its perks, and sometimes it had its drawbacks. Chastising himself, Sayd drifted back through the wall and watched the Exorcist move off into the hallway, returning to where the chase through the second floor had started.

Frustrated, the Exorcist decided to return to his office and give it some thought. Obviously, following the poltergeist was not bearing the fruit he had hoped. Sayd watched from the distance, smirking as he imagined the man's frustration at not being able to find a person who was following him. Now he knew his target would head back towards his lair, and it was only a matter of time now.

The Exorcist moved across the atrium looking back and forth as he looked for witnesses. When he looked back Sayd faded into the wall, watching his victim through the eyes of a poster. Now the Exorcist approached a door to the left of the cafeteria, taking a key from the pocket of his cassock.

"Ah," Sayd nodded. "I've got you now. Let us just see where that door leads before we decide how I am going to get a peek into your lair."

Sayd waited a few minutes and then drifted across the atrium in ghost form. He stepped through the door and found himself standing in the middle of a scissor lift, staring off at the darkness towards a set of stairs. What, he wondered, was at the end of those stairs? There was only one way to find out, and up Sayd went. At the head of the stairs was a door, and when Sayd peeked in he found the Exorcist sitting at a desk that overlooked the cafeteria. And now Sayd knew exactly what he had to do.

Back out in the atrium, Sayd entered the

cafeteria. He moved across the room towards the stage, knowing he was in full view of the Exorcist. As he slipped through the curtain, he turned back. Again only his eyes were visible as he looked up, watching the man in the window that lay halfway up the wall. What will you do now, my dear man?

Sayd didn't have long to wait. Soon the Exorcist disappeared from the window and moments later he entered the cafeteria. The man had taken the bait, and now it was time for Sayd to do his own disappearing act. Waiting only long enough to know the Exorcist intended to follow Sayd in behind the stage, the poltergeist drifted through the wall and into the kitchens of the servery. From here he continued until he was back in the hallway, where he doubled back to the entrance of the cafeteria and the strange utility closet with the staircase at its back end. If he were going to explore the Exorcist's lair, it was now or never.

"Oh what fun we shall have, Sayd my boy," he murmured as he stepped inside by walking through the door.

The stairs remained dark, as they had on his first trip up their length. Inside, the office was equally dark, but darkness had never bothered Sayd. He moved to the desk and sat down with a satisfied sigh.

"Now let's see what papers you have," Sayd spoke to himself. "I'm particularly interested in that list of names you are always studying. Whose names might I find there? My own, perhaps. Maybe even Portia, Lacy and Rhys?"

The search for the list was a short one. It lay on top of the desk, tucked underneath a blotter. Not a very clever place to hide it, given that almost everyone with a desk and a blotter tended to do the same thing with important papers – like a password list. This one was more interesting and far more legible. Some of the names were on a list he and his companions were compiling, a list of students who had already disappeared, or who they suspected would soon be transformed into monsters. The others, he knew, were those that the Exorcist suspected of being Recovery agents sent here by the Ministry of Magical Artifacts. His name had been scribbled at the end of the list, although Lacy's name was typed in near the very top.

"So you know about Lacy and I do you?" Sayd mused. "But nothing of Rhys and Portia. That means you will be making your move soon, so if we intend to turn the tables on you, we'll have to do it soon."

Sayd continued his search without uncovering much of interest. His equipment might have been amusing if they did not scare the poltergeist so much. These, he knew, were meant to harm him and creatures like him. Better they are left alone for the moment. Now, he thought, it was perhaps time to return to their lair and fill in the others. He wondered if they would believe him this time.

Chapter 32

"Boo!" Sayd cried, sticking his head up through the floor a few paces ahead of the Exorcist.

"Did you just say Boo?" The Exorcist raged, tossing a handful of salt towards the insolent poltergeist.

"It's what us ghosts do," Sayd poked his head through the floor behind the Exorcist and then disappeared as he spun on his heels.

"I'll ghost you," the Exorcist threw more salt.

Sayd stuck his head through the wall a few feet away. "You know, I learned this from one of the Human's viewing portals. The hunter never gets the rabbit. I'd give this all up if I were you."

"I am neither a human nor a hunter," the Exorcist punctuated each word with a handful of salt, peppering the wall. "And I always get my poltergeist, ghost."

It was night and the two had been at it for several hours now. This was becoming a nightly ritual over the last few days, the Exorcist chasing the poltergeist through the deserted halls. Despite the others' warning, Sayd was enjoying himself. He could keep this up indefinitely. He was one of the undead, and the undead needed no sleep. Not so for the Exorcist, who was rapidly tiring of their game. It was time to rethink their nightly romps, time to turn to tables and use the poltergeist's arrogance against him. And the priest thought he knew exactly how to do it.

After chucking a few more handfuls of salt at the poltergeist, the Exorcist turned in disgust and headed back to his lair. Sooner or later, the poltergeist would return to bedevil him, and when he did Sayd would find a surprise waiting for him. A very pleasant surprise, the Exorcist thought. At least it will be pleasant for me. What the poltergeist might think of it was another matter altogether.

Back in his office the Exorcist needlessly locked his door. Locked doors meant very little to a poltergeist but they gave the man a sense of security he might not have otherwise. Alone at last, he sat back with a sigh. A wicked grin suddenly lit his face. In a few more days all this would be over and he would return to the Otherworld to enjoy his well-earned fortune. Four agents, banished from life forever, and all thanks to the overconfident poltergeist. He reached down and patted the sack of salt his contact had purchased for him, gathering the strength to start his final chore for the night.

"And now we shall begin," he slapped his knees and stood up.

This would take some patience and a lot of preparation. First, he slit open the top of the sack of salt and took out a scoop from the black medical bag he always carried. With this, he patiently began drawing circles on the floor with the salt, careful to leave a narrow trail free of salt so he could move back and forth without disturbing the all-important circles. Once the perimeter of the circle was broken they were no longer effective against poltergeist or any other creature, so the path back to his desk would become important over the next few days. But laying the circles and the path was only the beginning of his preparations, for he must learn their location with enough confidence to move back and forth even in the dark.

"And now it is time to test myself," the Exorcist decided.

For the next hour, he walked back and forth from his desk to the door, carefully placing his feet so that none of his steps disturbed the delicate rings of salt that lay everywhere in his office. Satisfied, he flicked off the lights. The Exorcist paused, reviewing his path in his mind before he attempted it. Perhaps he was not as confident as he had thought, perhaps he was merely tired after pacing for so long, yet such meticulous preparations were part and parcel of his life as an exorcist. He was long inured to the rigours of such a life, to the long hours of preparation needed to trap and banish those from the Otherworld.

He walked from the door to his desk, where he turned on a light to study his path. Not a grain of salt had been disturbed.

"And now, my dear boy, we are ready."

Once again the others did not believe him when he told them about the Exorcist and his office, so here he was, on his own on the way to beard the dragon in its den. In the end, all he had managed was to start another big fight that left everyone not talking to each other. So, what else could he do? Sayd would have to deliver the Exorcist all wrapped up in a bow. Even then, some of them – Portia and Rhys – would spend most of their time scolding him for going out on his own. It was a no-win situation, but at this point what choice did he have? It was either the Exorcist or Lacy and him.

Which was probably why Rhys and Portia didn't care. It was not their names on the list, not their covers that had been blown. As Portia had said, 'if you two would pay more attention to your surroundings, no one would suspect you were not normal students.'

Here he was. The Exorcist's lair lay through a door and up a flight of stairs. Sayd paused to collect his courage. He had not done anything this dangerous since the night he died, dining on human food. And that was on a dare and not so much voluntary as this night's foolishness.

"Okay boy," Sayd told himself. "It's now or never."

Sayd drifted through the door and then remembered he was a ghost who could move through solid objects. There was no need for him to climb all those stairs and risk being heard during his approach. He would go through the floor, Sayd decided, and surprise his victim as he sat at his desk. Grinning wickedly, he walked through the stairs and into the space behind, judging where the desk would be in the office up above. Why pop up behind him when he could come up in the middle of the desk and grab the Exorcist by the throat? Still smirking over his own cleverness, Sayd began to drift up towards the floor.

The poltergeist made it halfway through the floor when he got stuck. Looking up, he saw the Exorcist standing over him with a wicked grin. "Got you!"

Chapter 33

"Where has Sayd got to?" Lacy asked.

The other two pretended not to hear her, turning their shoulders as they went back to activities they were only pretending at. Rhys was writing a letter home but had gotten no further than Dear, and Portia had been reading the same page since last night.

"Well, if none of you are going to help," Lacy huffed, "I'm going to go out and find him myself."

Lacy slipped into her room and grabbed her pack and a shock stick. Ever since Portia had come across those three insectoids Lacy didn't feel safe walking in the school at night without one. Especially if she would be walking the halls alone, and as she paused hopefully to see if the other two had changed their minds she knew she would be on her own. Finally, with a sigh, she turned and left the lair.

In the library, Lacy turned towards the window. It was a starlit night without a cloud in the sky. The brightness made her shiver, and she turned towards the comforting darkness waiting for her in the atrium. It wasn't too bad, she thought to herself, I walk here all the time and in the middle of the day at that. It was the knowledge that somewhere out there was an exorcist with her name on a list that gave her the heebie-jeebies. Who knew, he could be hiding behind one of the pillars or around a corner, waiting for some hapless passerby to leap out and do his worse. Not that she really knew what an exorcist did besides banish people. Even the sound of it sent chill banes running up and down her spine.

"Now, where would Sayd go?" Lacy said.

The last time he went out for a walk he had wandered into the girls' change room so Lacy turned towards the gym. Not that these would likely be open, but she did not think that mattered much to a poltergeist. It was a forbidden place, the type of thing that attracted a poltergeist like crows to roadkill. And so off she went her trusty lockpicks in hand, ready to check out both changing rooms with full expectations of finding the missing Sayd.

Rhys stretched with a yawn. "I think I might go for a walk and clear my head. Funny though, Lacy saying Sayd is missing."

"He never listens," Portia snorted. "He's always wandering off in a snit, no concern for our cover or our mission."

"You're probably right," Rhys said. "He'll turn

up sooner or later. I thought I might stroll down by the tech hall, do you want to come along?"

"Naw," Portia said. "I think I'll finish up my book."

Nodding, Rhys slipped into his room to fetch his pack and a shock stick. Maybe he would run into Lacy if he were fast enough. Feeling about as ready as he'd ever been, he slipped out of the lair and into the library. He too noticed the brightness of the night with a bit of a shudder, but now that he had set his mind on a task, he had no time for romance. Out in the atrium, he turned right, increasing his pace as he crossed the open space for the comforting darkness of the hallway.

Sayd liked to poke around in the tech rooms, Rhys reasoned, fascinated with Human devices as he had always been. Sometimes he would spend hours in there when the school was empty, turning on all the machines and listening to them chug along for hours. Sometimes he stuck his head inside the machines as they were running, sending sparks flying across the dark room. Rhys had accompanied him once and watched him do this, and he had to admit the effect was quite dramatic. Apparently, human machines did not like being messed with, and unable to talk, they exploded instead.

With his trusty lockpick set in hand, Rhys headed out towards the manufacturing classroom, one of the places he knew Sayd liked to go when he slipped out of the lair at night. Confident he would find the poltergeist, he lengthened his stride once again.

Alone in the lair, Portia set her book down. It was funny that Sayd was missing. Now that she thought about it, she hadn't seen him since last night, when he had come back to the lair with some fantastic tale about tailing the Exorcist throughout the school. How could he have followed an Exorcist anywhere? Those creatures could sense anyone from the Otherworld from a hundred feet away, so any attempt to follow him was doomed to failure before it started. So, that meant he was off sulking somewhere and Portia thought she knew where he was hiding. She remembered him telling her something about the space behind the stage, a place you entered through the music room.

Suddenly Portia decided she would go and have a look. She headed to her room and came back out with her pack. As a witch, she didn't need a shock stick for protection. Her hexes were protection enough. She stepped into the library, pausing to notice the brightness of the night with a frown and headed out towards the music room. Portia didn't waste her time with a lockpick set when a good glare and a hex would force any door that stood in her way. Once she was through the door and into the space behind the stage she was sure she would find Sayd sleeping in some hidden corner.

Forty-five minutes later, the three slumped back into the lair and collapsed onto the couch. None of them returned with Sayd.

"I went out for a walk," Rhys said. "Headed off down towards the tech hall. Funny I didn't see Sayd around. None of you happened to run into him?"

"I felt like a walk myself," Portia stretched like a cat. "Wandered into that space behind the stage. I didn't see Sayd at all."

"Well," Lacy huffed, "I went looking for Sayd down by the gym. You know how he likes to play in the change rooms, making everyone scream. I didn't see him there either."

"Shame!" The Mixmaster cried. "Shame on all three of you!"

"What's with you?" Rhys grimaced.

"What's with me, he asks," the Mixmaster sniffed. "I've been around the Academy forever. I have seen all the great teams come and go, and now I must witness this. Portia's mother and her companions who rescued a power stone from the Tower of London, the great Swashbuckler himself and his companions, who risked everything to bring back the Talisman from the Black Hole of Calcutta itself. And then you four, who think you can do it all yourself. No, Rhys, Portia, Lacy and Sayd refuse to work as a team, and now one of their own is missing, either captured or dead. Oh, the shame of it all!"

Portia sighed. "He's right. If we are going to find out what happened to Sayd, we are going to have to start working as a team instead of competing against each other."

"What are we waiting for," Rhys caught up his shock stick and his pack, "let's get going!"

"Perhaps you might want to take a moment to plan," the Mixmaster suggested. "Perhaps over a nice cup of floating toad's eye soup?"

"No time!" Lacy called, racing to catch up with

the others. "We have to find Sayd before something terrible happens."

"Me and my big mouth," the Mixmaster muttered. "Now what am I going to do with all this toad's eye soup?"

Chapter 34

A moment later, the three came charging back into the lair, having realized they could not go off until they were fully prepared. They had to face facts. Finding Sayd would most likely bring them face-to-face with the Exorcist, and they would need to plan and prepare a trap beforehand if they did not want to share Sayd's fate.

"You know," Lacy said. "Sayd did mention an office that overlooks the cafeteria. IIc said he followed the Exorcist there and discovered his lair."

"Yeah," Rhys nodded. "I kind of remember something like that."

"What kind of things scare an exorcist?" Lacy wondered.

"We need a Vok, a wolf symbol, or a Stanisa stone carved with runes," Portia said. "I know I have some in my pack. Now, where did that evil thing get to?"

All three had made the mistake of placing their packs down as soon as they had entered the lair, and now they had run off and hidden themselves.

"Have either of you ever noticed this office overlooking the cafeteria?" Portia asked, bending down to look under the couch.

"Can't say that I have," Rhys stalked across the room to check behind the grandfather clock.

"Me neither," Lacy gave chase as her pack came yipping out of a corner, running between Rhys' legs and tripping him up.

"I think we're going to have to check the whole school," Portia leapt at the strap of a pack, and it turned, biting at her with large teeth. "Ah, Rhys. I think I found your pack. It's over here."

Suddenly, all three bags made a break for it, running pell-mell across the living room and bringing all three owners together in a collision of arms and legs at the centre of the room. And as quickly as it had begun, all three had disappeared.

"You know," Portia rubbed her head. "These bags were fine when we were students, but now that we are agents, I think we need to replace them with something more serious."

Rhys rolled over and climbed to his feet. "I think you're right. I know we are going to need the net in my bag – it's the only one lined with lead – and I can't come close to that misbegotten backpack of mine."

"Well I think little Stinker is cute," Lacy said. "And I would never replace him in a thousand years."

"Not even for a series 8000," Rhys challenged.

"Something designed by Grundel or even Machiavelli?"

"Well," Lacy hedged. "A girl does like to look good. Maybe I'd pick up one of those for more formal occasions."

Finally, the three cornered their bags. Not wanting to have to fight for their equipment when they needed it, each began to fill their pockets for things they thought they might need in their confrontation with the Exorcist. Who knew when an ivory hairbrush might come in handy, or a mirror designed for looking around corners or helping pluck one's eyebrows. When they were done they dropped their bags onto the couch and headed out the door of the lair, leaving its safety far behind.

"Where to first?" Rhys asked.

"Up to the second floor," Portia decided. "There are a lot of hidden offices along those halls that none of us have ever been in. We'll do a room-by-room search if necessary, but let's start with those offices first."

The others nodded, confident they would find something up on the second floor. After all, they had already checked most of the ground floor. Out in the atrium they paused, glancing briefly towards the cafeteria before heading off towards the nearest stairway. Together they climbed up to the second floor and paused. The hallways looked so different at night, bathed in pitched black and empty of the yelling students and harassed teachers. They had chosen the middle stairwell closest to the main office and now stood kitty-corner from the bathrooms, trying to decide where to go first.

"There's a doorway down in the far hallway that I've never been through," Rhys said. "Maybe we should give it a look."

"Sounds like a good place to start," Portia nodded. "From there we'll work our way back here and check the doors down by the Chaplain's office."

"Do you think we should check in the chapel?" Lacy quavered.

"Not even an Exorcist could enter a chapel and survive," Rhys decided. "They may look like human priests but there is nothing holy about them."

Satisfied, Lacy led the way down the hallway they were facing and took the first right. It was funny that there was a doorway in the middle of the hall that seemed to lead nowhere. Rhys was confident they would discover the Exorcist's lair behind these doors. As they reached them, the vampire pulled out his lock picks and reached for the door, only to find that it was not locked. Shrugging, he held it open and let the two steps inside ahead of him.

Joining them, he studied the hall. "What's in that room?"

Lacy peaked in through the window in the door and shrugged. "It looks like a classroom."

Across the hall, Portia zapped the lock and pulled open the second door. "This is a classroom too. In fact, it has a second door that we passed in the other hallway."

"How about these stairs?" Rhys asked. "Does anyone know where they lead?"

The other two shrugged. With a shrug of his own, Rhys led the way down the dark stairway. At the bottom, he found himself in a large, dark space that seemed vaguely familiar.

"Oh," Lacy sighed, disappointed. "It's the automotive classroom. Didn't you already check in here, Rhys?"

"Yeah," Rhys turned and headed back up the stairs, the other two following.

"Let's head back and check out those other offices," Portia sighed. "If we don't find anything up here, we'll head down to the first floor and check there."

The doors near the Chaplain's office were no more fruitful. One led up to the roof, one led into a copier room, and while the third one was indeed an office, there was no one there and no sign of the Exorcist. From here they followed the hallways, finding several bathrooms, and a couple more offices, but again no sign of the Exorcist.

"I guess we should have stayed on the first floor," Rhys breathed. Come on, the main stairway is this way."

In the atrium, the three slipped into the cafeteria, searching its walls. On impulse, Lacy looked up at the rear wall that faced the stage. In the darkness, she could barely discern a window up near the ceiling. "Hey look! Is there an office up there?"

The other two spun around and followed her finger up to the window. "I think we've found Sayd's mysterious office."

Chapter 35

Now that they had found the office the three were at a loss as to how to access it. Where was the door? They moved from one end of the wall to the other without finding anything and even held the emergency open while Rhys checked outside. Nothing. Moving outside the cafeteria, they looked along the brick wall and came face-to-face with a door they had never noticed before.

"What's in here?" Rhys wondered out loud.

"Let's check it out," Portia suggested. "Maybe this is the way up to that little office."

Rhys took out his lock picks and quickly unlocked the door. As he opened it, they came up against a lift that blocked their way.

"It's just some kind of storage room," Rhys groaned.

"Look!" Lacy pointed. "There's a stairway in the back."

Portia shrugged. "Let's check it out."

Crawling up over the lift, the three fought their way through the junk blocking the way and onto the stairway. They looked up into the darkness, wondering what they would find at the top. Rhys shifted his grip on the shock stick, girding himself for a confrontation with the bogeyman of the Otherworld. He glanced at his companions, who nodded, waiting for him to lead the way. Still nervous, he stepped up onto the first stair and began to creep up the length of the stairwell. On his heels the others followed, the three bunching up for comfort and to shore up their courage.

"It's another door," Rhys whispered. "This must be it."

Rhys took out his lock picks when Lacy reached over and tried the door. It opened. She pushed her way inside, stepping into the office and into a trap that sprung like a cat. Suddenly Lacy found herself caught up in a webbing of silver chains, one snapping shut around her neck like a collar and leash around the neck of a dog.

"Ah!" She cried. "Help!"

"No! Wait!" Sayd called out from the darkness, but it was too late.

Portia stepped forward to help Lacy when something gave her a hard shove. She fell forward and tumbled into an iron maiden. A moment later, the lid slammed shut and she was locked inside, unable to use her magic.

"Hold on girls," Rhys said, gingerly stepping around Lacy.

And in doing so, Rhys tripped over Sayd's head

that was stuck in the floor. He stumbled backwards into a corner, where a horseshoe of garlic waited. Suddenly a shower of cloves fell from the ceiling, completing the circle and trapping the vampire inside.

The Exorcist and the Principal stepped inside, wicked grins plastered on their faces.

"Ah, and my trap has caught a few strays I see," the Exorcist cackled.

"You'll never get away with this!" Portia snapped.

"Ah, but I already have." The Exorcist laughed. "But do not worry, I will not leave you here to suffer for too long. My preparations for you are almost finished. All I really needed to see was what type of creatures you are, and now I know."

"Now what?" The Principal asked.

"Now," the Exorcist led his companion back out the door, "we head back to my workroom to finish a few items. What we have here is a vampire, a witch, a werewolf and a ghost – all four of whom are easy enough to dispose of if you have the right knowledge."

The two men stepped down the stairs and out into the atrium, where the Exorcist led the way towards the trophy case. As they came up to it, he turned and waved his hand at the Principal, looking for the key.

"What are we stopping here for?" The Principal asked. "I thought we were heading to Manufacturing to finish the apotropaics?"

"Yes," the Exorcist nodded. "We just need that pure silver cup. It's the only way to eliminate a werewolf."

"But that's our trophy from the Junior Olympics," the Principal objected. "Can't we use that second-place trophy from the golf team?"

"It's cheap metal," the Exorcist said, "no good for our purposes. We all need to make a few sacrifices, and I'm afraid this one is yours."

From here the men continued to the other end of the school and entered the Manufacturing class. The first thing the Exorcist did is to bring the silver cup to the workbench, where he had a puddling furnace heating up since they had left to check on their traps. He placed the cup inside and waited, his companion watching longingly as the cup slowly melted. As it lost its shape, the Principal reached up to his eyes and wiped away a tear. It was a steep sacrifice to make to rid his school of four meddling monsters, one he did not know if he was willing to make, although it was too late now.

"No worries, my man," the Exorcist consoled, "when those four our gone you can easily replace this one with many more."

The Exorcist decanted the melted liquid into a sand mould, shaping it into the point of an arrowhead. This he would beat and shape when it cooled enough, sharpening its blade to a point that would pierce the toughest hide. While he waited, he turned on a lathe and placed a rod of hemlock wood inside. With this he would form a stake which would take care of the young vampire, leaving only the poltergeist and the witch to eliminate. Both these would be more difficult to banish than the first too, one involving salt and fire, the other needing iron chains and water.

"Is there a pool around here?"

"No," the Principal shook his head, "not at this school. There is one at the school behind us, but I think they have security guards at night."

"No matter," the Exorcist said. "We'll have to use one of the sinks in the big kitchen. Fitting her in will be a bit difficult, but with a few cuts and a little leverage we should be able to get her done."

Chapter 36

"Another fine mess you're got us into, Portia," Rhys complained bitterly. He stood in a circle of garlic, standing on his tippy-toes to avoid stepping on any of the cloves.

"Me!" Portia stormed. "This was your plan, not mine."

"How was it my plan?" Rhys said. "You were the one who said let's go, not me. When I said we should storm the office, I was just joking."

"I don't see anything funny," Lacy scratched at the silver collar around her neck, "unless we were supposed to be the butt of your joke."

"Oh shut up," Rhys sneered. "No one asked you to stick your nose in this."

"Fine," Lacy sniffed, retreating to the other corner of the room.

"You shouldn't snap at Lacy like that," Sayd said. "It wasn't like she was the one who led us up into this trap."

"And if you had stuck with the group," Rhys

retorted, "and not gotten yourself trapped, we wouldn't be here in the first place."

"Well," Sayd sniffed, "if any of you had bothered to listen to me we could have figured out what these two were up to before they set this trap."

"Maybe Sayd is right," Portia said. "He did tell us he thought these two were up to something, but at the same time, Sayd, you have been wandering off ever since we got here, and most of the time getting into trouble."

"I'm a poltergeist," Sayd shrugged, "it's what we do."

Lacy sniffed the air, scenting something interesting. As the other three kept arguing, she dropped down onto the floor sniffing. Something was definitely interesting down here on the floor. Lacy picked up one of the white bulbs that surrounded Rhys and brought it up to her mouth and gave it a lick. "This tastes pretty good."

"Well Portia," Rhys was saying, "I didn't see you slowing down. In fact, you were stepping on my heels the whole way up the stairs. Ew, Lacy, what are you eating?"

"Garlic."

"Ugh!" Sayd cringed, "don't eat that. It's gross."

"Your right," Lacy decided. "It needs salt."

As she began to scrape the garlic cloves through the circle of salt surrounding Sayd, he turned back to his argument with Rhys and Portia.

"Only to try and slow you down," Portia said.

"Yeah, in your dreams maybe," Sayd laughed.

"Oh, look who's talking," Portia snorted. "This

is all your fault anyway. If just once you had listened to one of us, we wouldn't be in this mess."

"Ha! That's a hoot," Sayd said, "who's the one who never listens to anyone else. I told you these two were acting suspicious, but no, the witch and the vampire know everything!"

"Watch it, ghost boy," Rhys snapped. "We'd listen to you more if you weren't always acting like a moron. Oh, look, I'll just poke my head through a wall and take a peek in the girl's washroom. What harm will that do to our undercover operation."

"I just wanted to see what it was like in there," Sayd simpered. "Besides, it's not like anyone noticed."

"Oh, right," Portia laughed. "That's why all the girls were screaming at you to get out."

"And if you hadn't grabbed my shirt," Sayd snapped, "I wouldn't have gotten stuck."

"Oh, come off it," Rhys said, "you're always getting stuck."

"It's the metal," Sayd complained, "all these human buildings have a lot of metal in them, and I'm not used to it."

"He's right," Lacy said through a mouthful of salty garlic. "There is a lot of metal in this building. They don't even real fire for their lights. They must trap tiny fairies in these glass tubes or maybe real tiny fireflies."

"What do fairies and fireflies have to do with the mess we are in?" Portia demanded. "And quit talking with your mouth full, it's gross."

"Sorry," Lacy raised a hand to cover her mouth.

"Leave her alone already," Sayd snapped. "It's

not like she's hurting anyone."

"That's easy for you to say," Rhys glared. "You all know that the smell of garlic makes me feel ill. How would you like it if I started to eat some Brussel sprouts?"

Sayd rose up and faced the vampire, ready to throw down. "You would bring up Brussel sprouts, you overgrown leech!"

"Who are you calling a leech?" Rhys demanded. "You freak of nature. Who chokes on a brussel sprout anyway?"

"It was a dare!"

"Hey, you guys," Lacy looked up from her meal. "How did you free yourselves?"

"If you're free," Portia's voice came from the iron maiden. "Leave off with the male bonding and get me out of here."

"Yeah," Lacy scratched at her neck, "but first, could you please take this off of me. It itches like crazy, and I can't reach the last few cloves of garlic."

Realizing they were free and that time was of the essence, Rhys moved to free Portia while Sayd struggled to remove the silver collar from around Lacy's neck. Now that they were free they could turn the tables on the Exorcist and his erstwhile ally.

"If we hurry," Portia said, "we can resupply and get back here before they do."

"Yeah," Sayd urged, "we can ambush them. What's that old saying? We'll hoist them with their own petard."

"What's a petard anyway?" Lacy asked, leading the way out of the office. "It sounds like some kind of nasty-tasting vegetable."

"I think they were some kind of bomb," Portia said.

"We're not going to use a bomb are we?" Lacy frowned. "Blowing up the school seems a little extreme don't you think?"

"I only meant that we would turn the tables on them," Sayd said. "You know, trap them in their own trap."

"Oh, I like that much better," Lacy nodded. "And I'd like to fit that nasty Exorcist with a collar and chain of his own."

"I think what this really needs," Portia decided, "is the crystal prison the Ministry supplied us with. Once we have the two in there we can contact our control for a pick-up and get ourselves back home where the world makes sense."

The others nodded, more than ready to put an end to this mission.

Chapter 37

"Quick!" Lacy urged. "Let's get out of here before they return."

Untangling themselves from the ropes and chains and rings of salt, the four stumbled out of the office and onto a narrow flight of stairs. The bottom of the stairwell was a tangle of scissor lifts and miscellaneous stored here by the custodial staff. In the dark, they bumped and stumbled and tripped over almost every piece of equipment before they managed to tumble out into the atrium and scrambled towards the library and their lair.

"Hurry," Portia huffed, "we need to get ready and come back to the office before they do. That way we can ambush them."

At the doorway the Mixmaster was waiting, anxiously hopping from one set of legs to the other. "You are late. You must be thirsty. After a hard day's work there is nothing more relaxing than a mug of carrot juice and battery acid tea."

"Not right now," Lacy said and added as the Mixmaster's mouth began to droop. "Maybe later. Right now we have to hurry and get back as soon as possible. We found the Exorcist and the human who is selling the Abalaxia 47!"

"Oh, you'll want to take me along," the Mixmaster perked up. "Capturing villians is thirsty work, and everyone will need a smoothie or two to keep up their strength."

"I think it would be better if you stayed here and take care of the lair," Portia suggested politically. "We need to pack light and move swiftly."

Portia's bag danced at her feet, opening its mouth and sticking out a velvety pink tongue. It liked nothing better than packing.

"I'm sorry," Portia said. "I'm going to use this smaller bag the humans gave me. I think they call it a knapsack."

"Whhhaaa," her bag gave her a hard look.

"Because I don't have to fight with it to get my stuff back," Portia glared.

Her bag spat out an old tennis shoe, hitting Portia in the shin.

"Hey! That's my old gym shoe," Portia scolded. "I thought I lost that months ago. See," she snatched up the shoe and shook it at the sulking bag, "this is what I'm talking about. I had to scrub pots in spell class for a week thanks to you!"

"Are you coming or what?" Rhys asked.

"I just have to grab the unholy water," Portia called. "Lacy, don't forget the Cayan pepper."

"Oh, right," Lacy said. "Which one is it again?"

"It's the red one," Portia replied.

Lacy opened the cupboard where they stored their supplies. Like dogs, werewolves were colour blind, and while she had trained herself to see red, she could not tell one shade of red from another. She grabbed the first bottle of red powder she came upon and turned to shove it into her pack. She found her man-eating plant standing on her bag, trying to worm its way inside despite the obvious size difference.

"I'm sorry," Lacy soothed. "You can't come with us. Besides, silly, you wouldn't fit in my pack. How about you stay here with the Mixmaster and help to guard the lair?"

Its shoots drooping, the man-eating plant moved across the room and stood sulking in a corner.

"We can play when I get home," Lacy said. "I promise."

As Sayd turned to help Lacy with her pack, the Mixmaster jumped into his pack, twisting and turning to get himself hidden behind a vial of liquid and a jar of grasshoppers. Unfortunately, his cord trailed out of the pack, giving his position away.

"Oh no you don't," Sayd pulled at the exposed cord, dragging the Mixmaster from its hiding place. "Portia asked you to stay here and watch the lair. Who else are we going to leave in charge?"

"Of course," the Mixmaster stood up taller. "I was merely checking to see if you had forgotten anything. After all, this isn't my first mission you know. I've come to the Human world once or twice before you know."

"You'll have to tell us about that," Rhys patted the top of the Mixmaster.

"Shall I brew a cup of swamp water and pickle tea?" The Mixmaster asked hopefully. "There is nothing like a mug of swamp water tea when listening to a story."

"Not now, big guy," Rhys replied. "But we will as soon as I get back. Tea and a story, I promise."

Portia's bag wrapped itself around her feet and constantly tripped her as she tried to move about the lair to gather up last-minute items. "Can you please go and wait with the Mixmaster? I already told you that I'm not bringing you. We need to hurry out before the villains return."

"And then what?" Lacy asked.

"Yeah," Sayd said. "Where are we going?"

"I say we barge in there and confront them," Rhys said. "Bam! We take them down like the OWP SWAT team."

"Yeah," Portia retorted. "We'll just roll on up on our armoured brooms and let loose with the pepper spray and unholy water. Give it a rest, Rhys. We need to use our brains not our brawn. If we hurry, we can get there before they do and lay a trap."

"Trap, with what?" Rhys snorted. "Our only chance is to burst in on them and catch them by surprise. Slap them in the crystal ball before they know what hit them. Besides, there's no way we can go toe to toe with them with these toys."

"Rhys has got a point," Sayd said. "It's not like they've trusted us with any of the real powerful apotropaics. Most of these will only irritate a human, and I doubt any of them will do much against an exorcist."

"Either way," Lacy said, "we need to get back into the office. Why don't we figure it out when we get there?"

"Are you crazy?" Portia demanded. "You can't go busting into the lair of a human who knows of our existence without a plan. You learn that in your first year of the academy. You always have a plan and a backup plan."

"Then can you hurry up and tell us your plan," Lacy urged, bouncing up and down. "We can't stand here all night."

"It's simple," Portia sighed. "We sneak up to the office, and we catch them by surprise. Unless it's empty. Then, we set a trap for them."

"How is that any different from my plan?" Rhys demanded.

"Yeah," Sayd echoed.

"Easy, we're not bursting in before we know what's in the office," Portia said. "Besides, if we charge up the stairs like a herd of elephants, they're going to hear us and we'll be the ones who are surprised."

"How about we decide when we get there?" Lacy suggested. "At this rate, those two will die of old age before we get there."

Still bickering, the four raced out the door. The Mixmaster and his companions watched the closed door hopefully, knowing that their masters were not coming back for them. Disappointed, he turned to the others with a shrug.

"I don't like their odds without us," the Mixmaster sighed. "They can't even agree on a plan."

"Uhm mumble, bumble," Portia's bag replied through a mouthful of socks and a textbook.

"You know," the Mixmaster considered, "you really shouldn't talk with your mouth full. It's not polite, and you could choke."

"Mumble bumble shuffle bumble," Portia's bag complained.

"I know you are the bag of a teenage witch," the Mixmaster said. "and that your mouth is always full, but still, it's rude to talk with your mouth full."

"Mumble! Mumble bumble!"

"Well, yes," the Mixmaster conceded. "I do think it would be rude to ask you to never speak. How about a nice cup of battery acid tea? Just the thing to sip on when you are having a deep philosophical discussion."

Chapter 38

Quietly, Portia and her friends crept up the stairs leading to the office overlooking the cafeteria. This late at night the stairwell was a pool of darkness that hid everything from sight.   Bathed in pitch blackness, Portia led the way up, feeling the walls on either side with her fingertips. Behind her, the others fingered their weapons as they rose towards the office, where they were sure the Exorcist and the Principal waited. They were all nervous. None of them had ever used an apotropaic against a human and did not know if they would work. Most of it was things like balloons filled with Cayan pepper and pentagrams of lead or tin, and now that they were about to face one down, their doubts began to creep in with each step.

Who knew if these apotropaics even worked? Portia thought to herself as she lifted a foot to the next step. It was definitely darker and creepier on these stairs at this time of night. Everything was so quiet that if the others did not keep pressing up against her back she would think she was alone. And at that moment, she felt alone with her fears and doubts. An Exorcist was the boogie man that their parents had threatened them with as children, and now they were about to face off with one who had already proven dangerous. It had been less than an hour since they had escaped from his clutches, and now they were about to turn the tables on him – that is if the equipment they had been given by the agency even worked.

Portia reached the door and stopped, swallowing in an audible gulp.

"Okay, on three." Rhys teased.

"Three," Portia threw open the door and leapt inside.

"Ah-ha!" Sayd cried at the same time as the Exorcist. "We've got you now!"

"No you don't," Lacy objected, "we ambushed you first!"

"No you didn't," the principal corrected. "We let you walk into our trap. Since we prepared our trap long before you did, we've ambushed you."

"Yeah," Sayd retorted, "but we knew you were lying in wait for us here, and we intentionally sprang your trap. So we've ambushed you!"

"You young punk!" The principal snapped. "I'll teach you to talk back to your elders. Have a taste of my holy water."

A vial flew through the air and shattered on the wall behind Sayd. Flinching, he waited for the burning to start. When it didn't, he stood up and licked his lips. "You know that this doesn't work unless it's been blessed by a saint, and I'm guessing you're rather short on saints around here. My weapon, however, is much more effective."

Sayd through a balloon stuffed with a red powder at the exorcist and the principal. It burst into a cloud of dust that had all of them sneezing.

"What is this?" The Exorcist demanded.

"Cayan pepper!" Sayd shouted triumphantly.

"Tastes like paprika," the principal licked some of the red spice off of his finger.

All four turned to look at Lacy, who shrugged. "Well, they are both red."

Meanwhile, down in the lair, the Mixmaster 3000 was pacing back and forth across the kitchen counter.   He turned to the Grandfather clock, glaring. "I don't like it. Our young masters should not have gone off alone to confront an Exorcist."

Chanting, the Grandfather clock replied, " As I have said, said, said…I am in total agreement."

"They should have called a Magical Mobile Assault Team," the Mixmaster continued as if the Grandfather clock had not spoken. "What are we doing, just standing around here." He whirled on Portia's bag as it attacked the edge of the couch, trying to swallow it.

"Oon't nooo," it mumbled through a mouthful of couch. "wat?"

"I'll tell you what we should be doing," the Mixmaster said, "we should race off and rescue them, that's what we should be doing. You there! All curled up asleep in the corner! What kind of man-eating plant are you? Huh! Who's going to feed you meet when our masters are gone? I tell you, it won't be me."

"But isn't that your function?" The toaster ventured. "Aren't you a food processor?"

"No, you fool!" The Mixmaster barked. "I am a drink dispenser of the first class, trained at the Academy to serve future agents of the Magical Recovery Agency.   And I for one refuse to sit around while some villain threatens my master. Who's with me!"

The other items in the room stared up at him before turning to look at the walls and the ceiling, many of them making small coughing sounds.

"Come on, guys," the Mixmaster pleaded. "We're we not made to serve? Are we the type of appliances and baggage that sits by and watches the dust grow on us?"

Portia's bag spit out the corner of the couch and asked, "will I get to bite something?"

"Yes! That's the spirit." Mixmaster cried. "Bite to your heart's content. Bite their shoes, bite their shins! Who's with us?"

"Mumble, grumble, bumble, Mama Kabush," the man-eating plant complained.

"I'm going to take that as a yes, big guy," Mixmaster enthused. "Anyone else?"

"I'd come," the Grandfather Clock mumbled, "but my rheumatism is acting up, and besides, I haven't been wound in several days."

"Sorry," the toaster cried, heading off towards the nearest cupboard, "I have to wash my elements. Crumbs, you know. They get everywhere."

"Well," Mixmaster said, "no matter. We three are off to glory. Come on, you two, we have masters to rescue. Tonight, we meet our destiny."

"And I get to bite him, right?" Portia's bag asked.

"Uhm," Mixmaster looked at it askew. "Sure. Help yourself."

Mixmaster tottled out the door, throwing a glance over his shoulder to check that his companions were still following as he continued to pontificate on their bravery. A custodian paused, rubbing his eyes as he watched the strange trio creep across the atrium. Looking again, and still seeing the odd parade of plants and appliances he rubbed his eyes a second time. He turned to the vacuum cleaner he had dragged down the hall with him. It watched him with the two decal eyes and smile, making no move.

"Stay here," the custodian muttered. "We have work to do." Shaking his head, he continued to mutter to himself. "I must be working too much. No more nightshifts for me. I'm transferring to the day shift."

Upstairs, Sayd squared off with the principal, who held up a silver cross. "What's that?"

"A cross," the Principal cried. "Stand back!"

"Again," Sayd shook his head. "I'm a poltergeist, you know, a ghost. Not afraid of crosses, silver or otherwise."

Sayd held up his own apotropaic.

"What's that?"

"A lead pentagram," Sayd replied. "Everyone knows humans are afraid of magic, and the pentagram symbolizes magic. Besides, lead is poison to humans."

"Only if we eat it," the Principal snorted.

"In that case," Sayd held out the pentagram. "Care for a bite?"

"No thank you, I've already eaten." The Principal put away the cross and pulled out something from another pocket. "But take this."

"Garlic?" Sayd reached out and grabbed a couple of cloves. "Don't mind if I do. Once again, ghost, not afraid of garlic. In fact, I am quite fond of it."

"Enough of this foolishness," the Exorcist snapped. "His toys may be harmless, but I assure you mine are not."

The Exorcist held up what looked like an oversized blunderbuss and pointed it toward the four agents. Sayd ducked behind Portia, who tried to hide behind Rhys as he ducked behind Lacy. Lacy stood her ground, confused.

"What is it?"

"The ultimate apotropaic" the Exorcist crowed. "It fires a mixture of my own design, guaranteed to banish all spooks, creeps, vamps, and werewolves. It contains salt, silver nitrate, holy water, and of course, slivers of the Holy Rood."

"What's so rude about it?" Lacy retorted.

"Not rude," the exorcist snapped. "Rood, as in the True Cross."

"Well, that's just rude."

He raised the blunderbuss and took aim, adjusting the barrel as the four scrambled for cover. Just as the exorcist was pulling the trigger, the Mixmaster and his companions burst into the small office.

"Hold on, Masters," he cried, firing a stream of yellow liquid across the room, "we're here to rescue you!"

Behind him, Portia's bag and Lacy's man-eating plant struggled into the room. The yellow liquid hit the Exorcist in the face, drawing the barrel of the blunderbuss up towards the ceiling.

"My eyes!"

"Uck!" the Principal cried. "What is this stuff?"

"Lemonade," the Mixmaster said. "What? Did I put too much sulphuric acid in it? Maybe I should have added a little more rotten lemon peels?"

Portia's bag spat something at the principal, bouncing it off his nose. An overdue library book followed, but the exorcist managed to dodge it as he rubbed at his eyes and reloaded the blunderbuss.

"Hey!" Portia cried. "That's my hairbrush. You told me you didn't have it!"

The bag shrugged and spat out an old running shoe.

The blunderbuss came up again, its barrel wavering as the Exorcist aimed through burning eyes and blurred vision. The four danced from side to side, trying to keep one step ahead of the deadly weapon, their motion adding to the confusion in the small office. Suddenly, and tentacle of vine and leafs reached out and wrapped itself around the Exorcist's waist, pulling him towards the door as the blunderbuss thundered, sending a shower of salt, silver nitrate and bits of wood into the ceiling. A second shoot stretched out and wrapped itself around the Principal until both were immobilized within a tangle of leafy vines.

"Quick!" Portia called to her bag, "spit out the orb."

"Ah-ah," the bag shook its top half no and backed away.

"Get it," she yelled to the others, diving across the office towards the bag.

Sayd jumped to block the door and landed in a tangle of vines as the man-eating plant forced itself further into the room, trying to swallow the two struggling villains that it had trapped in its vines. As Sayd stepped out of this tangle, Lacy and Rhys dove after the bag. They collided in the middle of the room, the bag running through their legs as their heads slammed together. The three managed to drive the bag back towards Portia, who dove headfirst onto the floor, catching it up by its drawstring. Choking, the bag was dragged backwards as the four struggled back to their feet.

Grabbing its pink silk tongue, Portia scolded as she yanked, "spit it out! Spit out the orb this instance or I'll turn you into a toad. And this time I mean it!"

"Na-num-na," the bag complained, vomiting out an overdue library book and a dog-eared book report from two semesters ago.

"Give it up," Portia seethed, "you raggedy hunk of shoe leather!"

"Mine," the bag sulked, spitting out a shoe that bounced off Portia's nose.

"I know," the Mixmaster suggested, "how about I fix the bag a nice cup of sewer water and lime tea? Would you trade the orb for a sewer water and lime tea?"

The bag paused, thinking. "Nope."

"What if I threw in a dash of fish scales?" The Mixmaster wheedled. "Everyone loves a sprinkling of fish scales"

The bag spat the orb at Portia and leapt out of her grasp, bouncing up and down beside the Mixmaster as it waited on its tea. Portia glared at the bag and scrambled after the orb, wondering if she could sell it off to become a goblin's chew toy.

"I got it!"

"A snow globe," the Principal scoffed.

"It's not a snow globe," Portia stood, holding the orb out with one hand, "it's a magical orb."

The man-eating plant screamed as his prey was ripped out of its shoots, but not as loudly as the cry of the Principal as he was swept up in a magical vortex. "If you don't stop this, I will give you detention for the rest of your natural life!"

"You forgot that part," Lacy moved to settle her pet plant. "You know, all about detention and stuff."

"Oh, yeah," Portia held out the orb again. "I arrest you in the name of the Magical Recovery Agency. If you have anything to say in your defence, save it for the judge."

"A little too late," Rhys laughed, "don't you think?"

"Well," Portia glared, "at least it got said."

Chapter 39

It was done. The sorcerer lay locked safely away in a crystal, which was securely packed in her bag, waiting to be transported back to the Otherworld. Portia stood at the door of the room she had shared with Lacy, inspecting their secret lair one last time before the four caught the bus and left the human world behind. Somehow she expected more fanfare at the end of her first mission. Okay, maybe not a parade, but at least something. Maybe a representative of the council or one of her superiors showing up to let them know they had done a good job. With a discontented sigh, Portia turned and moved off to join her companions in the main room.

"Well," Lacy was saying, "what now?"

"We pack up and meet the bus on the roof," Sayd dropped his bag at his feet with a dull thud. It turned and stuck a leathery tongue out at him in a loud raspberry.

"We should celebrate," Portia suggested.

"Oh yes," the Mixmaster said, "and I have a new recipe that is perfect for the occasion. Chocolate and fermented lemon rinds, with just a dash of swamp water."

"Chocolate?" Rhys questioned skeptically.

"Oh, it's something I picked up from the drink dispenser in the cafeteria," the Mixmaster frowned. "Not much of a talker, but very helpful. Not all Mixmasters will share their recipes."

"What the heck," Portia said, "you only live once. A round for the house."

The Mixmaster hummed and hawed, screwing up one of its eyes as he set to work. Lights blinked, grinders whirled, and steam leaked from a dozen ports. The Mixmaster began groaning and moaning, opening one eye to make sure the others were watching him work. When he was sure they had seen how hard he was working over his latest creation, a bell rang and a clay mug began filling with a frothy liquid.

"Well," Lacy laughed, "it was your idea. Go ahead and taste it."

Portia screwed up her face and reached out for the mug. Blowing on the hot liquid, she tentatively took a sip. "Hey! This isn't half bad."

"It doesn't need a tad more rotting lemon peel, or perhaps a skosh more arsenic?" The Mixmaster asked anxiously.

"No," Portia reassured him, "it's actually quite good."

Satisfied, the Mixmaster worked busily making

three more mugs of his chocolate concoctions. Soon all four were settled amongst their luggage, sipping on mugs of hot liquid with one eye on the clock. None of them wanted to miss their bus back to the Otherworld, fearing they would be trapped in this crazy mortal world forever. That, or become the laughing stock of the Recovery force. Having to be rescued on your first mission would be hard to live down, and no doubt end their careers before they even began.

"Portia!" Lacy cried. "Are you feeling okay?"

"Yeah, why?"

"Girl!" Lacy said. "You're turning purple."

"You're one to talk," Rhys laughed, "Pink Lady."

"Yeah," Portia sneered, "Well, you're looking decidedly green."

Sayd turned, trying to catch his reflection in the shiny surface of the refrigerator, but like vampires, poltergeist did not cast a reflection.

"Don't bother," Rhys said, "you couldn't get much more orange if you tried."

"Oh God," Portia moaned, "it's not coming off. I look like a grape or something."

"It's probably just an allergic reaction to mortal food," Lacy shrugged. "It ought to wear off eventually."

"Let's hope soon," Portia glared at the Mixmaster, who busied itself with an innocent whistle. "If we show up to the academy like this we'll be the laughing stalks of the Other World."

"No time to worry about it now," Sayd said. "Our bus will be here any minute now."

Together they grabbed up their bags and tumbled out the door of their lair. Portia turned, taking the time to dismantle the lair, turning to her bag and struggling to put the pyramid inside.

"No!" Her bag complained. "Too full!"

Frustrated and in a rush, Portia gave her bag a boot and stuffed the pyramid down its gullet. Yanking the tie closed before it could spit anything out, she dragged it behind her as she raced to catch up to the others. Without stopping to check if the coast was clear, the four tumbled out of the library and began running across the atrium.

"Hey!" The custodian cried. "What are you kids doing here?"

"Run!" Rhys urged.

With their baggage waddling behind them, the four raced towards the front door and out into the night. Without looking back, they scanned the roadway for their bus and found it hovering above the same tree they had landed on when they had first arrived. Still running and pulling their baggage behind them, they crossed the street and came to a halt beneath the branches of the tree. Rhys scrambled up into its foliage, turning to catch their bags as the others threw them up to him. One by one, he threw each into the bus before turning to help the others scramble up the tree. Portia grunted and groaned, thinking that witches were not built for climbing trees as Rhys pulled her up and the branches and leaves slapped her in the face.

When Lacy and Sayd joined her on the bus, Portia turned to help Rhys on board with Sayd. He was still hanging half out the door when the bus started up and shot into the air.

"Wait!" Portia cried. "Rhys is not on board yet."

"No problem," the driver gave a rictus grin. "I can fix that."

The bus tipped to the left and all three came flying onto the bus, where they landed on Lacy in a heap of limbs.

"Everyone take a seat now!"

The driver shot straight up into the night sky and the four flew backwards into the bus, colliding with their baggage as they landed somewhere near a seat. Climbing out of the tangle and onto a seat, Portia settled back and gripped the bottom of the seat to avoid another flight through the rear of the bus. The others untangled themselves from their baggage and scrambled onto seats as the bus shot through a series of loop de loops and swooping dives. Without the longer arms of their owners, their bags flew threw the ground, bouncing off the rear doors and the heads and shoulders of the four in their wild flight through the interior of the bus.

"Where did they get this driver?" Lacy complained.

"Barnstormer," Sayd gulped, raising his hands to avoid bouncing off the front of the seat. "He and his brothers used to terrorize the countryside with their biplanes."

"Bloody haunts," Rhys muttered.

The bus began climbing straight into the night sky, throwing them back against their seats as the skin on their faces was pulled back by the g-forces. Up and up it rose, the moon filling the front window until it looked as if the crazy driver would not stop until they left the atmosphere. And then the bus dropped into a steep dive. Portia and her friends were thrown forward so violently that she almost toppled over the back of the seat in front of her. Trying to stop her momentum, she had no hands free when her bag came flying forward to clock her in the back of the head. Dizzy from more than the motion of the vehicle, she somehow managed to right herself when the bus tilted onto its side, throwing all four and their luggage out of their seats.

Once his passengers were dislodged from their seats, the driver popped the back doors and tilted the bus back until his passengers and cargo were deposited onto the ground. Portia rolled away from the heap and stood groggily on her feet.

"What now?"

"Now," the driver cackled, "it's time for your debrief. See you next mission."

"But I'm purple!" Portia wailed.

"At least you're not green," Rhys replied sardonically.

"I like it," Lacy said. "I look pretty in pink."

An ancient goblin shuffled towards the group, corralling their luggage and lifting it under one of his long, hairy arms. "This way, masters and mistresses."

Portia turned towards the ancient goblin and frowned. He was pointing towards the headquarters of the Magical Recovery Agency, the last place where she wanted to be while she was still purple. With a sigh, she shuffled forward, matching the goblin's slow pace. Behind her, the other three fell into place, moving as reluctantly as Portia towards a meeting with the vampire who would one day be their superior. For Rhys, it was worse, because this vampire just happened to be his older brother – the one of his twelve siblings who was closest to his age. This was the first time he would see Wrathgar since his older brother graduated from the academy, and he was currently a sickly, fluorescent green. And knowing this made Portia feel better about her own predicament because sometimes the knowledge that someone else's circumstances were worse than your own gave you perspective.

Still not totally relieved, Portia entered the building behind the goblin. The Recovery agency was a new building, its granite walls not yet blackened with age, and soot from the many torches and lanterns that lit its interior had barely marked its walls. It stood amongst its neighbours like a shining beacon, a symbol of justice that had inspired Portia in her youth to follow her mother into the Ministry of Magical Artifacts. Now she wished she had chosen to become a spellcaster or went to work in a magical ingredients factory – anything that would not bring her here to this moment, approaching the office of the Director of Field Agents with her skin and hair glowing purple.

"They are waiting for you inside," the goblin croaked, sketching a bow before shambling off into the darkness of the hallway.

"Well," Lacy said, "we might as well get this over with. The worse they can do is send us back to the Academy, and that's where we're going anyway."

The others nodded and then gathered behind Portia, waiting for her to lead the way inside. Gulping, she pushed open the door and fell through it as the others pressed inform behind, their luggage tumbling in after them. Behind a small wooden desk, a banshee sat powdering her nose, a compact held in front of her face so she could squint at her complexion in its cracked mirror. Looking up, she noticed the for and pressed the intercom.

"Your nine o'clock is here," she squeaked.

A small bat flew out of the intercom box, flying into the office beyond through a glass tube. A moment later, the four heard it mimic the receptionist's voice with the exact pitch, timbre and intonation.

It flew back and replied in a whiny, bored voice.

"Then by all means," it said, "send them in."

Again the other three and their luggage crowded behind Portia and she was shoved through the second door before she was ready.

"Well," a fussily dressed vampire asked, brushing at an imaginary speck of dust on his sleeve. "What do you have to say for yourselves?"

"We're back from the Mortal world," Rhys offered.

"I can see that!" Wrathgar sniffed. "Is that all you have to say?"

"We found the ones who were smuggling the Abalaxia 47," Portia said.

"Yes," Lacy added. "It was an exorcist and this evil human called a Principal."

"And he tried to kill us," Sayd insisted, "the exorcist, not the human."

"And was he the one who turned you those dreadful colours?" Wrathgar demanded.

"No," Portia shook her head. "That was the Mixmaster 2000."

"And this Mixmaster," Wrathgar pressed, "he was involved with thisAbalaxia affair?"

"No," Portia and Lacy insisted before Portia added, "the Mixmaster was in our lair. He wanted us to try a new drink to celebrate the end of our first case.   And,   well…"

"End of your first case?" Wrathgar snorted. "It doesn't seem as if you have accomplished anything, let alone solve the case."

"Oh, wait," Portia stuck her hand into her bag and it hastily closed its mouth, trapping her there. With one foot holding it down Portia rooted around inside before pulling her hand free, the crystal orb prison in her hand.

Wrathgar took it, holding it with two fingers. He gave it a vigorous shake, asking, "and who's in here?"

Inside the crystal orb, Allan stroked his long blonde tresses while Tara gave her thinning head a confused scratch. Across the table, Benita glared at his boyfriend. Wait, he thought, my name is not Benita.

"It's the exorcist and the principal," Rhys said. "We captured them."

"Ah, I see." Wrathgar waved a dismissive hand. "Well, don't you have somewhere to be, like the Academy or maybe a shower? I wouldn't be seen out in public in those colours."

Outside the office door, Sayd turned to ask,

"was he throwing shade at me? Because I feel like he was throwing shade at me."

"He was right though," Portia said, reaching into her bag, "we don't want to be seen in public looking like this. I have some spare robes in here somewhere."

She pulled out a second orb and looked down at it with a troubled frown. "I forgot they were in here. Oh no! You don't think we gave him the wrong one, do you?"

Rhys shrugged. "What does it matter? Whoever is in those orbs is not getting out any time soon."

Chapter 40

Wrathgar held the globe with two fingers, frowning down at it in disgust. With the tip of his pen, he lifted the lid of an iron chest and dropped the globe inside. Taking a silk handkerchief from his shirt pocket, he scrubbed imagined dirt from his fingers, the same look of disgust on his face. When he was done, he carefully cleaned his pen before returning it to his pocket. Pressing a button on the intercom, he called his receptionist.

"Thelma, can you send someone in to take care of this," Wrathgar paused to seek the appropriate word, "thing."

A tiny bat flew along a tube connecting the two intercoms, and returned a moment later, perfectly mimicking his receptionist's voice. "Right away sir."

Some minutes later a timid knock sounded on his door. Irritated, Wrathgar looked up and snapped, "Well, come in already. Do I have to make every decision myself?"

A stooped-shouldered ancient goblin with bushy white eyebrows shuffled into the room. He raised one of these bushy eyebrows at the vampire but said nothing. He knew he would get yelled at whether he knocked or not.

"Well," Wrathgar demanded. "Take it away."

"Where?"

"I don't know," the vampire huffed. "Delta six."

Deep six, as those who worked in the vaults referred to the lowest level of the facility, was reserved for the most dangerous items. Anything placed in this section of the vault would never see the light of day again. Frowning, the old goblin lifted the iron chest from the desk and tucked it beneath one arm as he turned and shuffled out of the office. Nodding to the secretary on his way past, he continued his journey along the hall to the service elevator that would take him down beneath the surface, where the vaults lay in a thick carpet of shadows.

At the back of the building the hallway grew darker, the torches flickering and smoking more than in the office area, where the hallways saw more traffic. Set against one wall was a steel door that led into the service elevator. The ancient goblin adjusted the weight of his burden and reached out to push the call button. A small bat squealed and shot off into the dark shaft, entering the elevator car in a cage marked with a number that corresponded with the floor where the call button had been pushed, where it gave another squawk. Inside the car, a stooping troll nodded and began pulling on ropes to bring the elevator up to the main floor of the building.

"Morning, Ralph," the ancient goblin nodded as he entered the elevator.

"Morning, Sam," the troll's deep voice boomed. "Where to?"

"All the way to the bottom, I'm afraid," Ralph held up the iron chest. "This one is to be deep-sixed."

The troll nodded. "Must be something dangerous. Hate to go down that far myself. You sure you don't want me to hold the elevator until you return?"

Ralph paused, thinking. "Guess I would. Strange things happen down that deep. Wouldn't want to be stuck waiting down there. Never know what might happen."

"Was it true old Herman was turned into a hideous monster when he got trapped down there?" Same asked. "I heard he came out looking like a vampire, all cleft chin and straight teeth and long straight hair."

"Heard the same thing myself," Ralph nodded. "Heard they forced him upstairs because of it. Nobody wanted to work with him."

"Do you blame him?"

The elevator car settled into the bottom of the shaft with a clunk and a bat squeaked to let them know they had reached their destination. "Good luck."

Ralph nodded and shuffled off into the darkness. Goblins were born and bred in the depth, where light was non-existent or dim at the best, but even the ancient goblin did not like the sinister air down in the depth of the vault. He shuffled forward with the iron chest tucked over one arm, keeping his eyes down on the floor, because, for goblins, what they could not see could not hurt them. A lifetime of habits was hard to break, and when you were part of an underclass in a class-conscious society, many of those habits involved avoiding notice.   Still watching the tiles on the floor, Ralph reached the shelves at the far end of the room. Sliding the iron chest onto a middle shelf amongst the dust and shadows, he turned and shuffled his way back towards the elevator.

And so, here the Pens of John Paul II lay, waiting for their next adventure. Stay tuned for *Pens in the Otherworld*.   Just as soon as they free themselves from this iron chest. Does anyone have a bobby pin? Maybe a crowbar close at hand?

ABOUT THE AUTHOR

The Pens of John Paul II is a novel-writing course where young writers participate in creating a novel. This year we had several young writers:
Tara O'Shea
Benjamin Rosevear:
Ranah Omar
Elliot Tharby
Nelly O'Neil
Karlee Myres